Memories
- A Novella

The Hilarious Nightmare of Growing Up

notionpress.com

Memories - A Novella

The Hilarious Nightmare of Growing Up

Soumya Mukherjee

Notion Press

Old No. 38, New No. 6
McNichols Road, Chetpet
Chennai - 600 031

First Published by Notion Press 2016
Copyright © Soumya Mukherjee 2016
All Rights Reserved.

ISBN 978-93-86073-75-4

Dedication

This book is dedicated to Pragya and Parmita, who made this happen despite my innate inertia.

Contents

Contents

Acknowledgements

I thank my long suffering family, especially my wife, who have heard these anecdotes umpteen times and still pretended to laugh at the jokes.

I thank Jug Surayia of TOI, who published the first story I sent out to the big bad world, and all subsequent stories I sent to him.

I thank my young tech savvy colleagues and friends who patiently guided me and carried me through the maze of technology involved in writing a blog.

I thank the numerous readers from all around the world who read and occasionally claim to like my stories on the blog, especially the gentleman from Moldovia, which I had to search for in the atlas. Your generous comments made me take this plunge.

I thank professor Koshy who invited me to the nanowrimo competition from which this book is born

I thank Author Sirish Singh who prompted me to follow his example and publish through Notion Press.

Finally I thank in advance all you readers who have spoken with their wallets and bought the book, and also those who have borrowed it from their friends

Edited by

Pragya Mukherjee

Cover and Illustrations by

Parmita Mukherjee

Prologue

B oy had just realised what makes it all worthwhile.

The agony and ecstasy of dating, climaxing into the frightening and optimistic institution of marriage; the exhilarating and excruciating experience of fatherhood; the sheer joy and heartbreak of bringing up kids; seeing them grow up from the helpless baby to adorable toddler, hero worshipping child, irritating tween and insufferable teenager.

Boy had gone through the gamut with his elder daughter who had now entered college and exited the teens, and in her full time preoccupation with creativity, politics, activism, recreation, socializing and academics (in that order), had ceased to notice that parents exist. She however had handed over her unfinished task of educating papa to her younger sibling, who had just entered her teens.

She worked hard to make Boy a more sensitive, liberal, metrosexual, "with it" man, and root out all subconscious traits of the 'MCP.'

Quite used to constructive criticism, Boy was therefore extremely surprised to hear her wondering comment: "Papa, you can write!"

Investigation revealed that she had come across the friendly neighbourhood magazine which had carried a story by Boy. Flattered by being asked for a contribution, and too lazy to do anything new, Boy had rehashed an old published story, which was the one she had found.

Encouraged by her interest, Boy dug out an ancient scrapbook where he had collected copies of various "middles" published in Delhi dailies like TOI, HT and Express, mostly before she was born.

An engrossed half hour later, she came up to Boy and peremptorily ordered him to start writing again. This was the best criticism or review Boy had ever received.

So he wrote what he felt at that moment- "I have realised what makes it all worthwhile…."

The Rites of Passage

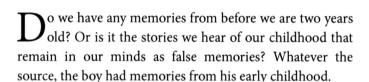

Do we have any memories from before we are two years old? Or is it the stories we hear of our childhood that remain in our minds as false memories? Whatever the source, the boy had memories from his early childhood.

The house with red cement floors, the very high ceiling, the vast veranda. He realised later that dimensions get expanded in childhood, size is relative. The perspective of a child is from closer to the floor. On visiting some of his childhood homes in adult life, he noticed how they had shrunk. But going back to his memories; he remembered cycle rickshaws, a canal, a white domed building which he later realised was a mosque, and strange wailing, which he now knows was the call for prayer, the Azaan. He remembers the white car that ferried his father to work, the parties at home, and most of all, his babysitter cum life-coach, whom he called Eda.

Unusually for those times, Eda was literate. This was before the advent of television, so he kept Boy quiet and well-behaved by reading to him. He did not read nursery rhymes or bed time stories, but rather whatever was available. It could be newspapers, classics, penny dreadfuls, mushy romances, religious texts, poems, or just about anything printed in Bengali and readily available. Both the boy's parents being

avid readers and cultured people, there was no dearth of reading matter. The boy loved the sonorous rhythms of the epic Mahabharata, set in rhyme in an archaic language, and whole passages would remain in his memory. When called in to the drawing room to be presented to guests and asked to recite rhymes, the boy would sometimes lisp off passages from the epic. Not knowing what the boy was spouting, and hearing an ancient language, a rumour spread that the kid had memories of past lives. The other by-product of this early indiscriminate indoctrination into literature was the boy's lifelong passion for stories, reading them, telling them, hearing them, watching them and even trying to write them. He grew addicted to strange tales of magic and mystery, history and mythology. The printed word held him in its grip, and the sound of language fascinated him. Words were his music.

They stayed in a small town in a relatively underdeveloped state in Eastern India, Orissa, where the boy's father was a big man and owned a car, one of the very few in that town. His father was very affectionate, but was a very busy man, and travelled a great deal. The boy's mother was a talented extroverted soul, very demonstrative in her affections. She was a talented musician and organised many cultural events and musical soirees. She was largely occupied in her cultural pursuits, so that the boy's closest companions were his babysitter and the chauffeur, Taji. Taji was the boy's rendition of Tahfeem Hussain, the chauffeur's real name, which was too much of a mouthful for a child. The origins of the nickname Eda is lost in the mists of time. Taji had only one story to tell, about three idiots, but he told it well. In fact, when the boy had grown up and had children of his own, Taji came to meet them and repeated the story for another generation, this time revealing that the three idiots had actually been the boy and his two brothers.

But we digress. Memories have this curious habit; they don't behave in an ordinary linear fashion. They have no respect for chronology. They keep leaping across time and space. I cannot decide whether to bring the boy's memories in line by the scruff of the neck or let them ramble and leap around with unbridled abandon. I think I will try Buddha's Middle Path, or the Grecian golden mean. Forget chronology, but try to maintain some semblance of order by linking topics as the memories jostle each other for attention.

Eda and Taji help fast forward the memories by a dozen years or so, to the boy's sacred thread ceremony. Having been born into the allegedly privileged caste of the twice born, the boy had to pass a rite of initiation at the age of fourteen when about to enter manhood, called the Upanayana. This ceremony is supposed to be a rebirth, thus the 'twice born,' and gave him the right to wear the sacred thread. He was initiated into the prayers, rituals and mantras that are the exclusive privilege of the Brahmins. The ceremony lasted three days, during which he remained interred in a room and conducted himself in accordance with strict Bramhacharya principles – rising at dawn, eating one meal a day (self-cooked Vedic food or fruits), meditating, praying, studying and collecting alms from the visitors. The kind of alms that visitors were wont to bring would make any mendicant leap with joy, as it involved wads of cash, watches, clothes, electronic gadgets, gift cheques and such stuff. In reality he read the numerous books he had received as gifts or 'alms.' The boy had especially asked for books, much to the relief of the guests. The alms giving guests were then treated to a feast that was far from Sattwik, and involved mutton and fish. The boy was disgruntled, but after prolonged negotiations was promised a grand treat after the three days of confinement and Spartan life.

On the list of his guests were his two childhood mentors, Eda and Taji. They had come to meet their old ward at considerable expense and effort, after taking leave from their current jobs. The boy was eager to meet them, but there was a hitch. During those three days he was not permitted to lay eyes on any non-Brahmin person. Not even the Sun is allowed in as the Sun god is a Kshatriya. And here there was a Shudra and a Muslim seeking audience with the young Brahmachari. This was an abomination. The elders and relatives would have none of this sacrilege. The boy was crestfallen. But he had a staunch supporter, his rationalist and strong-willed father. He decreed that the two ex-employees would meet the boy, and those who did not like it could lump it. The matter was referred to the family priest who was conducting the ceremony. He had already developed a rapport with the boy, who was curious about the meanings and significance of the rituals and prayers. The priest had been patiently explaining everything to the boy. The priest gave his verdict. A Brahmin is he who gives rise to good thoughts in the boy's mind. It cannot be decided by an accident of birth. These people have taught the boy in his childhood, and as Gurus, played the role of a Brahmin. They would visit him.

The impasse was cleared with what was in those days a revolutionary decision. It taught the boy rationality and consideration, and gave him the confidence to question doctrines and customs. It also taught him that not every priest was a hidebound conservative and religious fanatic as his leftist friends would one day claim. Rationality and intelligence are not anyone's sole preserve. The boy truly grew up that day.

2

Play Date

W e go back to the boy's childhood. But wait, it sounds
rather weird calling him the boy. This was what the
'burra sahibs' condescendingly called waiters in restaurants
in the old days when political correctness was unknown. Or
worse, what racist white colonial types called their darker
hued subjects. So boy goes, but the problem remains, what
to call him? His anonymity is important, as he represents a
milieu, not an individual. As a compromise, let's name him
Boy.

Boy was being taught to socialize. He was not yet four,
and living in that small town in Orissa. He occasionally went
on play dates to neighbouring houses with kids, especially
when their parents were not at home. He would have
preferred remaining home and having his babysitter read
to him, but sometimes the help had other chores to do and
were happier when the boy was not around. They lived in a
respectable middle class neighbourhood, which meant that
the people were mostly house owners who had lived there
for generations and could be counted upon being deeply
conservative.

The boy was a little frightened of the other kids, who all
knew each other and ragged the new entrant from an alien
state. He was also frightened of their parents, who pestered him
with many questions and said things he couldn't quite follow.

The way they sniggered made him uncomfortable. These people were curious and a little critical of their new neighbours from the big city and their strange ways. The boy's mother did not mix too intimately with these people. Her crowd was artier, comprising of professional musicians, amateur thespians and wannabe writers. She was a talented musician and writer herself, and organised many cultural do's and musical soirees. Some of the regulars later went on to become national and international icons in their fields.

But to the neighbours this was a bohemian gathering of mixed genders, where music, animated conversation and loud laughter could be heard. Eyebrows, therefore, were raised. Boy's father worked for a British company, and as per their corporate culture, an occasional cocktail party was thrown. People of various communities and both genders gathered, including a sprinkling of Europeans. Alcohol was served, music played, and who knows, maybe there was even dancing! Boy's mother, instead of condemning her husband's wayward ways, actually played hostess! The combined eyebrows of the neighbourhood almost leaped out of their heads. As they dared not question their younger, hipper and more affluent neighbours from the big city, Boy faced the brunt of their curiosity and disapproval. "What happens at those parties my child? Are coloured sherbets served? Does your mummy have them too? Do they dance? Do people fall down? Do those singers and young men come even when your papa is not around? What do they do? Are you sent away?" The questions only bewildered Boy. He could sense the implied criticism but did not understand why. He could not fathom why such normal activities inspired such prurient curiosity among the aunties. He resented the grilling but was unable to escape.

Boy himself thoroughly enjoyed the notorious gatherings, where he was much fussed over. He was indulged by his parents and remained the centre of attraction at these parties. He would even sing on stage, once accompanied by a flautist who is a household name today. Not everyone was enamoured by him though. An English upper class guest who believed like most of his generation that children should be seen and not heard, and should not be present at social gatherings for grownups, was annoyed at Boy's frankly expressed wonder at his height and commented on his poor manners. Noticing Boy's crestfallen face his father made it clear to the guest that this is perfectly acceptable behaviour in India. On other occasions he was the star of the show. His name was difficult to pronounce for foreigners, and once when he was asked to repeat it a few times, Boy ran and returned with a mug engraved with his name. As he had not started play school then and was yet to learn how to read, this quick wit was commented upon by the assembled guests, who pronounced him a genius. This was happily endorsed by the fond parents, and Boy grew up firmly convinced of the 'fact.' This supremely ill founded over-confidence, along with his addiction to stories, resulted in academic and later career performance which proved the exact opposite.

But we digress again. Although we had agreed that memory is an unruly self-willed beast, and is impossible to control, we must maintain a semblance of order. So we finally go back to the play dates. The kids played Statue, and they forgot to unfreeze him. Or they played Hide and Seek, where he was never found. When he was the seeker, the group escaped to some other house and he could find none, thus being left in the clutches of the aunties again who continued with the grilling.

Sometimes he was taken out by the canal to play cricket. He was told to stand in one place and not move whatever happened. He enjoyed this better, and stood and dreamed while the kids carried out strange rituals. He was told that he was a fielder or spectator or lamppost or whatever. The role suited him. One day, someone spotted a snake in the field. An alarm was raised and all the kids ran away. But none had remembered to call Boy. Boy was an obedient kid and stood firmly in place without moving until he was told to leave. He thought that this was some part of the mysterious ritual of this thing called Cricket. In any case he was used to being left alone when the other kids ran away. He also did not know what a snake was or that it was considered dangerous. He stood still and curiously watched the strange creature wriggling away. The snake may have been harmless, and in any case would not disturb someone unless it itself was disturbed, and soon disappeared. The other kids came back and berated Boy for staying there like an idiot. They made him promise not to tell his parents, which of course he promptly did, describing this creature called snake with great excitement.

The major gain from this adventure was the edict that he was not to be left unsupervised with the other kids. The babysitter was berated for his lapse and was told to shadow Boy at all times. The minus was that they decided to enrol Boy in a preschool kindergarten. This led to a whole new nightmare, as the boy was to find out over the years.

3

Going to School

Boy was taken one day to a strange building by his parents, where, after a bewildering conversation with a man in a funny white gown, he was left in the company of an ugly lady in a short skirt. This lady was to be called 'teacher' and the white gown was 'father.' This was confusing as Boy already had a father, who wore ties and suits, not funny gowns.

Boy wanted to cry, but was too petrified to utter a word. He was taken by teacher to a covered veranda, which was the kindergarten class. There he was stared at by a bunch of menacing looking boys and girls. On command, they drawled, "Welcome Boy" in a frightening tone. Boy sat down on the spot on a bench pointed out to him, and kept his eyes firmly on the ground, avoiding meeting any of the malevolent eyes.

Strange rituals were being carried out of which the boy could make little sense. Periodically everyone chanted something; it was all going on in what Boy knew was English, but which he could not comprehend at all. Teacher also made strange drawings on a blackboard with chalk, and the other children did something in their notebooks. Boy silently suffered through it all. After a while a bell rang and everybody ran out of the classroom yelling, ignoring the teacher. Boy was left alone in the room with the teacher.

But the teacher took him outside. His parents were waiting. The ordeal was over.

Slowly over time Boy got the hang of school. The chanting were rhymes which they had to recite, but which made no sense. The drawings were 'alphabets,' which had to be copied, but he didn't know why. The teacher recited the names of the children, and you had to say "Present Mam." Why this was done continued to be a mystery. The teachers spoke in English, and the children spoke in Oriya or Hindi, all of which Boy followed only sketchily. Somehow he muddled along. He was dropped to school by their chauffeur, Taji, but not in the car, which his father used.

His father loved to drive, and on his frequent road trips for business tours he took Boy and his mother along, as well as the baby sitter and chauffeur, Eda and Taji. His father always drove, with Taji and Eda in the back seat, and Boy in between both parents up front in their roomy white Ambassador car. These were wonderful memories. Boy was very proud of their spanking new car, so different from the funny looking older models around those days. They travelled this way throughout Eastern and Central India, staying in dak bungalows and circuit houses. These were ecstatic days for Boy.

But memory, the sneaky fellow, has wandered off again, and has to be dragged back to school by the scruff of its neck.

We left the boy going to school with the chauffeur, but on a bicycle! Boy loved the ride. Perched on the carrier or on the front rod, breeze ruffling his hair, chatting with Taji, this was the only good part of his day. He would often plead with Taji not to be taken to school. Taji would come again during break-time carrying his lunch. Once again, pleas would be made to escape back home. Occasionally this was accomplished, with Boy's mother's complicity. Sometimes the morning whining melted his mom, and class would be skipped. This cavalier attitude towards duty and routine, with early encouragement, became a deep rooted habit which played havoc with his academic and professional progress in the years to come.

In school he learnt the rudiments of writing, or at least the alphabet. But he did not copy out his As and Bs in neat rows as they were supposed to. His was a large standing A, then a host of little ones around the feet, in the gaps, climbing up the sides. The Bs could face either way, or lie down on their backs, or face down. This drove teacher nuts, and the other kids' copies were shown as examples, to little effect. Sometimes the letters would begin in nearly neat rows, but soon start meandering around like a river reaching its delta.

Boy also practiced his new art on the walls of his home. On discovery, his babysitter Eda was frantic and tried to clean it up. But Boy's mother, on seeing the new interior decoration, was thrilled. Leave alone punish him, Boy was fussed over by his proud parents for acquiring this new skill. Boy also learnt to repeat rhymes about some children who fell down and hurt themselves, mulberry bushes, and pleading for rain to go away, all of which seemed utter rubbish. But the worst was about an egg breaking. It had the word 'together.' This did not sound like English to Boy. It sounded more like Oriya, which, to his ears, sounded like someone gargling.

Boy loved the sound of the English language that his father spoke with his colleagues. He often imitated them by rolling a piece of paper, putting talcum powder in it, and blowing out 'smoke,' all the while sitting on a chair, legs crossed, going "Fush fash, swoosh, swish, ta da ha ha." 'Together' just didn't fit in. His attempts to correct the rhyme by substituting real English words didn't go down well with the teacher, who used the cruel punishment of asking another student, a girl, to twist his ear. The pain wasn't much, but the humiliation brought tears to his eyes, and worse, his anger, misery and tension made him incontinent.

He always tried to hold out, as he lacked the confidence to raise his hand and shout "Miss Toilet!" – the approved manner of requesting a break to relieve oneself. But now, control left him and he could feel a warm flood trickling down his shorts. Soon others noticed his wet patch and howling laughter and an angry teacher brought out the tears again.

Next day, he pleaded with passion to be allowed to never return to school again. He could not bear to face those horrible kids. Nor could he share the story of his humiliation at home. But to his relief, his pleas were acceded to, and his brief stint with formal education came to an abrupt end. The reason for this magnanimity was soon disclosed. They were moving to Calcutta!

4

Calcutta

The news created a sensation around their little neighbourhood. Boy's family was shifting to Kolkata, or Calcutta, as it was known then. It was the dream city for the kids around. Boy didn't see what the fuss was about, as they often visited Calcutta, where his mom's family lived.

In fact, he was a little scared, because on his last visit to Calcutta, as it was then called, he had witnessed a strange and scary spectacle – deserted roads and buildings on fire. It was called a Riot. He was apprehensive that Calcutta had riots. Later he was to witness many, and one changed the course of his life forever. But we will speak of that later.

Maybe the next chapter will be Riots. Right now I will force this undisciplined memory back to Cuttack. Oops, it leaked out. The original plan was to keep names, places and dates unspecified, as the story is about an era and a milieu, and the small town could be anywhere in India.

Boy was excited about a change of scene, and thrilled at the jealousy he generated in his tormentors. His chief prosecutor, a hard-boiled boy, declared "What's so great about Calcutta? I've lived there for years."

"Me too!" chimed in the others.

The leader elaborated, "When I was in Calcutta, I drove trucks," that being the most glamorous profession in the eyes of that gang.

"So did I!" declared a slightly older girl who resented his leadership.

"When I was in Calcutta, I wore bangles up to here," chipped in a little girl, whose new colourful glass bangles were her pride and joy, and who wanted the gang's attention to focus on it.

"When I was in Calcutta driving trucks, I wore bangles up to here," the older girl proclaimed, indicating her elbows, not to be outdone by the little miss.

But Bhombol, the leader, had to have the final word. "When I was in Calcutta, driving trucks, I wore bangles up to here," he declared, indicating his shoulders and leaving no room for further one-upman or womanship. He glared around at everyone, daring them to contradict him.

Boy of course believed everything he heard, and visualised these tiny boys and girls wearing turbans, driving huge trucks and wearing bangles up to their shoulders (As all truck drivers Boy had seen were Sikhs he thought that turbans were part of the uniform. Later, when his in-laws were of this turban-wearing faith, his pop in-law had shared a hilarious story about this popular Bong misconception, but again, memory is running haywire and will be dragged back). It was a surreal image, though that term was something Boy learnt years later.

The move happened, with promises of staying in touch that didn't, and they moved to his maternal grandparents' home in Calcutta till a more permanent home was ready.

It was a large house with red cement floors, green windows with latticed shutters and scary bathrooms that held the Boy's worst terror – cockroaches. He has never recovered from this phobia, though all others, like ghosts, vampires, bullies, grown-ups, riots, thieves, girls, exams and speaking before a crowd have long ceased their reign of terror.

Grandpa was a retired civil servant, the first native to hold several important positions in India and with the grand title of Rai Bahadur, who after decades of living like a brown Englishman had turned Bengali with a vengeance.

He exclusively wore dhoti kurtas, or 'Punjabis' as they are called in Bengali. He ate on the floor, sitting on ornate velvet mats called 'áshon' and off intricate metal dinner sets consisting of thalis or copper plates which looked like artwork. These thalis were always surrounded by dozens of batis or bowls, each containing a different dish. Meals were an elaborate affair. The men always ate first along with the children, and women followed later, with the servants eating last. The men merely tasted many dishes, the leftovers being finished by the ladies and servants, in that order. Children of course had first preference, and the boy reigned supreme.

An exception was made for Boy's father, who, in a suit and tie, ate half boiled eggs in a cup with toast, or poached eggs and tea, sitting at a table and chair specially set out for him. The top of the egg was sliced off, and the interiors scooped out after being sprinkled with salt and pepper. Boy desperately wanted to have that English breakfast, but could never articulate the wish. He ate luchi, a puffed maida poori fried in ghee, an exquisite delicacy, with fried vegetables and curry. Later, when he finally got to try the English breakfast, it turned out to be quite ghastly. Today, when he is condemned to bread and eggs for breakfast, he would kill for those luchis. One must be very careful what one wishes for.

The process of school admissions began afresh. He was subjected to another interview with 'fathers' in white gowns and teachers in short skirts for the label of a posh school. The boy stared blankly at the many questions asked in incomprehensible English. It was a lost cause till the principal, in his Irish accent, pointed out an aquarium with the question, "What is this?" A simple "Fish" was what he in all probability was looking for. But Boy had an aquarium at home and knew what it was called.

"Aquarium," he confidently proclaimed. Family lore has it that it was this aquarium that got him into the prestigious school. He spent the next thirteen years there, some of it happy, till he finally escaped to freedom and delinquency, with the confidence to think and fend for himself, at Delhi University. I, his creator, will carry on the saga of Boy, his roots, his experiments with truth and sex, and his discovery of himself and his place in the chaos of life. Please stay with me for the course. I will try not to disappoint you too much. Maybe you will see yourself here.

5

Roots

The boy's family moved out of his grandparents' sprawling traditional house and into a spanking new high rise apartment. Boy enjoyed the bird's eye view of his surroundings, the modern tiled bathrooms with showers and bathtubs, and especially the western style toilets. But he missed his grandfather, who had been his constant companion for the past few months. They used to go for long walks to the lakes, where Dadu, as Boy called his grandpa, showed off his savant grandson to his cronies.

Boy's father would bring him illustrated Russian books and tell him about the formation of stars, evolution of life, dinosaurs, early man, discovery of fire and other such fascinating stories. Years later, Boy would pay forward the debt by telling those stories to his children. Anyway, thus empowered, the boy interacted with his Dadu's friends.

"What are you studying these days, my child?"

"Darwin's theory of evolution," came the straight-faced reply from this kindergarten student. Thus the savant reputation took root.

Dadu too was a fund of stories. He had been a civil servant of the British Raj, often being the first 'native officer' to hold many senior positions, and had travelled and worked in many remote places. Boy was enthralled by his adventures.

Travelling on horseback and in boats, living in tents, wearing the sola toupee and khakis, encountering dacoits and wild animals, it all seemed a fairy tale. Boy admired the hunting rifles and service revolver which were showpieces now, but figured prominently in those thrilling tales.

His grandfather also told grim tales of the freedom struggle, which in his time of service, and against his own inclinations, he had been tasked to quell. He had great admiration for the armed daredevils, called 'terrorists' by his employers and 'freedom fighters' by his countrymen, of whom his own nephew was a part. He had scant respect for the congress-wallahs, who later usurped power and reaped the bounties of independence, and whom he called collaborators.

He however mourned the death of close friends and colleagues assassinated by these very boys, sometimes right in front of his eyes. A heroic episode in India's freedom struggle was what came to be known as the Verandah Battle, where three teenagers with pistols attacked the heart of British administration, the Writers' Building or the Secretariat, and held the forces at bay on the verandah till their ammunition lasted. Boy's grandfather was shot at at the very same battle, but that did not diminish his admiration for those fiery young men. But that is another story.

Memory, as she is wont, is taking off in tangents again, but before we drag her back to the linear model, could we take one little sidestep?

The deprivation of Boy's material comforts due to his intoxication with stories started early. His babysitter, Eda, had the difficult job of feeding him. This had to be accompanied with stories. To this day, Boy cannot eat without a book in his hand, unless in entertaining company. Sometimes a screen replaces the book, but the story has to be there. In any case, going back, Eda was soon out of stock as his repertoire was limited. So he used the simple scheme of eating up the meals himself, and presenting the empty plate to Boy's mother. Boy never snitched on his close companion, and continued to lose calories in exchange for stories. Later, he would lose grades, job opportunities and dates for this dangerous addiction.

Going back to the story, Boy spent hours peering from the newly gained vantage point of a 10th floor balcony. From there he saw a bus being burnt, a thief being lynched, and his first communal riot, scenes that would scar him for life. But that comes later. First we go back to his roots.

Boy's paternal grandfather, whom he called Choto Dadu for his short stature, was a very jolly gentleman with ever ready wit. He worked in the steel town of Tatanagar. Boy loved his visits to that town and the rides in Choto Dadu's ancient Austin. He too, was a treasure trove of stories, mostly funny, and as Boy later realised, sometimes made-up.

Choto Dadu's family came from a remote backward district of Bengal, where they were landowners in a village and were treated like kings. He called Boy 'Prince of Wales of Nowhere land.' How the family first reached the village was a typical colonial story. The tribal population there, in order to bring a priest for their temple, had invited an impoverished scholar from a famous Sanskrit college to their village. A few generations later, the Brahmin's progeny owned the village. But by the time Boy's great-grandpa was in charge, zamindari wasn't paying much in the arid land. This enterprising gentleman decided on a course considered sacrilegious for his class and caste – he started a business. But maybe genes can tell, and soon he went bankrupt.

Now he thought of something even more drastic. For landowners, employment was the worst dishonour. But he decided to pick his brightest kid, Boy's grandfather, to be educated in the city and choose a profession. Here too, he broke tradition. Gentlemen undertook a liberal education or at worst studied law. Medicine was borderline respectable. But he chose the new-fangled discipline of Engineering, and upon the completion of his son's intermediate studies, took him far away to the first engineering college in the country, in BHU.

However, the hurdles arrived as soon as they did. By the time they reached, admissions were over and the academic session had begun. Not willing to take no for an answer, he demanded and received an appointment with the Vice Chancellor of the University himself, the legendary Madan Mohan Malaviya. The VC explained the situation to the old man with an analogy he could follow, having come over by rail.

"The train has left the station and nothing more can be done," he said kindly.

But Boy's great grandpa retorted, "Why, you can always pull the chain to stop the train!"

The old man's ready wit won Boy's grandpa the berth, and changed the family fortune for good. The next hurdle became financing his education, which was solved by finding a match for the young man so the dowry could fund his degree and later higher education in England.

The financier of this unique scheme was one of India's first doctors, with a country practice, immensely rich, and who had replaced his traditional transport of a horse carriage with an imported marvel – a motor car.

Boy's father remembers his visits to this Doctor's mansion especially because of this car, where he idolised the chauffeur Ram, who wore a cap and goggles and had the glamour of an airline pilot. When asked what he would like to be when grown up, he had confidently replied, "Ram Driver."

Maybe that is what prompted him to drive his own car while letting his chauffeur rest in the back seat when he grew up, and further, what prompted Boy to constantly take off on impromptu road trips when he in turn grew up. Boy's first material possession would eventually be a car, even before he bought furniture for his one room apartment.

The patient reader will eventually hear those stories. Just stick with me.

6

Riots

There was a new game being played in the boy's school. It was called 'riot riot.' It was like Kings, or rather Bompat, which probably was a corruption of 'bombard' and consisted of hitting the opponent with a rubber ball. Kings was a slightly organised version with the last one escaping declared King. Bompat had no rules. Boy hated it. As a not very athletic, skinny, bespectacled bookworm, he was hit often and hard, and was amongst the last to be chosen in teams. Maybe that is why he overcompensated in his youth by becoming a delinquent, and in his middle age by taking unnecessary physical risks in trying to prove machismo.

But let us go back to the game. In Riots, the only difference was that the teams were made up of Hindus and Muslims. Occasionally football was played on these lines, but kids could change sides at will, and the Christians, especially the Anglo-Indians Chinese, and Armenians, were heavily in demand by both teams, being the most athletic. But this time it was merely hitting each other with the ball, every hit scoring a point. Moreover, slogans were shouted, "Allah hu Akbar" and "Har Har Mahadeo" or "Jai Kali." The Christians spread out over both teams with individual kids choosing the team where his buddies were.

The genesis of this game was a spate of communal violence that periodically afflicts different parts of India, depending on political expediency. Bengal is usually free of this malady, since that aberration of 1947, and then too, the Bengali populace of Calcutta were not active participants, merely collateral damage.

Around this time, an incident in faraway Kashmir over an alleged theft of a relic from a historic Mazhar had led to communal violence across the country and in Pakistan, both East and West. Anyway, some creative soul may have witnessed or heard of this madness, and the game was devised. This was the first time that Boy was exposed to the communal divide.

A few days later, trouble erupted in Boy's neighbourhood. Boy's high-rise was in an area which was declared Pakistan during the '47 disruptions. It had consisted of havelis of rich Muslims, some of whom had migrated leading to housing societies and this one high-rise cropping up, but the poor Muslims remained in a ghetto in the back streets, and were the factory workers and domestic help for their better off Hindu neighbours. That day, the battle lines were drawn between the area behind Boy's house, and the societies in front, the road in between being no man's land. Boy had a panoramic view of the proceedings, and heard the cries learnt in that game in school.

Although far away and apparently detached from the scenes of mayhem below, there was a sense of fear. He could also sense what some of the adults around him felt, that Muslims are bad people, to be feared, that they were the enemy. Boy thought of the kids in class who played in the other team, and couldn't figure out how X, Y and Z could be Muslims. A and B he could understand. And C, one of his great tormentors and the major force in the Hindu team, ought to be Muslim, he felt.

The Police arrived. Tear gas was employed. Even high up in the balcony the boy had to use wet handkerchiefs to avoid irritation. Soon the Police left under combined onslaught from both teams. Then the really scary army arrived, curfew was imposed, and a deathly peace was established.

Most of what Boy witnessed was much like the game, with projectiles being exchanged, though some of them were the exploding kind. But one scene traumatised him. A man on a cycle had blundered into a lane and was ambushed by a waiting mob. The body kept lying there through the day till it was removed by the army. It looked like a rag doll, lying forlorn in the street, in a dark pool spreading around him. This scene kept recurring in his nightmares.

Years later in Delhi, post Babri, he witnessed a similar scene in the street near his office where he was parking his car. A fish seller on a bicycle was set upon by four men, and lay curled upon the ground screaming for mercy while his ware lay scattered on the road. Boy felt sick to the stomach to see his nightmare materialising in reality, and his helplessness in being unable to do anything to prevent it. But perhaps the presence of the car saved a life, as the attackers soon ran off, and a while later, the victim got up and ran away in the other direction. Boy remained frozen, unable to move, till a police patrol car arrived.

But Boy saw the unspeakable horror of riots and felt the terror from up close for the first time in '84. The ruling family had allegedly given a call for pogroms against Sikhs, in retaliation the assassination of the Prime Minister by her Sikh bodyguards, and the capital burnt. Boy and his friends made desperate attempts to call the police or stop the insanity in their neighbourhood, only to meet dangerously hostile reactions. Trying to find shelter for a fleeing family proved futile, but they helped the family escape to another neighbourhood.

The rising smoke from all over the city, marauding bloodthirsty mobs, impassive policemen, buses being stopped to hunt victims, the scenes haunt him still.

The most surreal image to stick in his mind is of a man holding a life size baby doll from some looted shop by its legs, and swinging it as he walked by, the blond frilly dressed doll looking like a real baby's carcass being carried by a monster.

Boy worked with a volunteer group trying to rescue trapped families, bring relief to those taking shelter in camps and getting information on missing family members. The scenes and stories of horror leave a numb feeling, and can neither be remembered nor spoken of, like the woman in one camp who kept staring blankly, not speaking a word.

Perhaps that is one way to cope with unbelievable horror, and the reason why the survivors of the worst holocaust in our subcontinent, the survivors who left their homes in Pakistan to seek refuge in India, maintain a wall of silence, and little literature exists on any first hand experiences.

Tragically, in '84, many of those survivors of Partition faced another pogrom, in their country of refuge, from the very people they had thought were their protectors.

One close friend of Boy, a Sikh, made a remark that encapsulated the entire feeling of helplessness of targeted communities:

"For the first time I realised that we are a minority. All along I thought that minorities are other people."

Lost

The new school in the big city that Boy had joined was very grand, with a huge building, sprawling grounds, strict discipline and large classes with close to fifty children. It was run by an Irish principal and tended to by Anglo-Indian teachers. Teaching was exclusively in English, and speaking in vernacular was strictly forbidden. The boy was completely lost.

After being dropped off in the morning, the first challenge was finding the assembly hall, and then finding his class and section. After that he could just follow the group and hope for the best. During assembly, the white man in a white gown droned on about something, and then a dark guy in a white gown barked something, and finally everyone shut their eyes and roared something in a sing-song voice.

Boy understood the "Our Father," and thought of his father; then "Daily bread," which reminded him of his packed lunch, which, daily, was bread and butter, which he hated; and finally, "Amen," which meant that they could open their eyes and start shuffling off, in formation, following the teacher to their classrooms. The rest was gibberish to him.

Class was not much different. The lady would say things, and write stuff on a blackboard, and point at charts and pictures; but what it was all about was lost on Boy. He would follow the example of his classmates and take out random books and copies from his bag, doodle on them with his pencil, and put them back later. Sometimes the teacher would collect them, and return them later with red marks on them.

On many occasions he was made to stand up and was sternly spoken to, with much wagging of fingers. Sometimes, he would be asked to stay back after class to finish something. This overwhelmed him with an unnamed dread, helped along by a sadistic tormentor who filled him with stories of ghosts that appeared, and boys who were never seen again after detention.

Boy was certain that Eda, whose job it was to bring him back home, would go back upon not seeing him; he would get locked up in the school to become dinner for the monsters his friend had warned him about. This always made him start whimpering, to the amusement of his tormentor–a tiny curly haired brat. The kind-hearted teacher would then let him off, and the sight of his waiting babysitter would come as an immense relief, as another day of confusing torture came to an end.

Over some time, Boy managed to figure out basic reading and writing, could speak a form of Pidgin English, and had even learnt to vaguely interpret the Anglo-Indian and Malayalam flavoured English that was the medium of instruction.

But the one instruction that eluded him was, "Make sentences." What on earth was he to do? How do you make sentences? What is the correct answer?

His constant companion Eda perceived his tension, but could not help. He would ask Boy how the other kids figured it out, to which Boy would respond quite creatively.

"The answer is put up on the notice board, which is kept locked," he would reply seriously. "It is only opened for a minute and those boys who can rush up and read it know the answer. Also the monitor who puts it up knows, and tells his friends. And the teacher tells her favourites."

Some sort of embarrassment kept boy from involving his parents in his troubles. When the first assessment card was handed over to be signed by his parents, Boy's mother saw "1st term" on the cover, and immediately assumed her darling genius had come first in class. Only further perusal showed his rank, 50th. Not so bad, in a class of 50 students, and this was also mentioned on the card.

She however preserved all those assessment cards, and displayed them to Boy's own kids, thus ruining forever his moral authority to exhort his children into better academic performance.

Boy's homework continued to be in arrears, and his class work was always incomplete. Notes to parents remained unanswered, and for a good reason. The parents were unaware of them. Demands by teachers to meet the parents were artfully fended off – Boy would explain that his father was on tour and his mother did not talk to strangers. Storytelling came naturally to the boy from a tender age. Circumstances helped him develop a survival strategy. After the monitor collected the exercise books, including Boy's incomplete, incorrect or blank contributions, and stacked them on the desk, Boy would look for an opportunity to sneak up and quietly retrieve his copy. Next day's work would then begin on a fresh page.

Every day on the way to school Boy would pray fervently to all the Gods he knew, and the new ones he discovered in school, that his perfidy remain undiscovered, bowing his head to every temple, shrine or mazhar on the way, making the sign of cross for good measure. The statue of Mary in the school landing would get special obeisance from him, on the assumption that she would have greater control of fate within those premises. He would also watch out for occult signs like the number of sparrows spotted, as it was common knowledge that, "One was for sorrow, and two for joy."

But despite all these precautions and insurance, fate played nemesis one fine day. Boy had had no opportunity for the sneak retrieval of his offending notebook, when the teacher picked up the one on top of his, leaving the evidence exposed. Now nature played villain, and a whiff of breeze turned over the pages of his notebook.

The teacher was very surprised to view the results of this quite literal exposure, and examined the whole notebook. Then she proceeded to commandeer his schoolbag and study all the exercise books in it. Startled by her discoveries, she summoned Boy up front, and holding his ear in one hand, displayed his notebooks to the class one after the other.

This was followed up with further corporal punishment, which was not only legal, but commonplace in those unenlightened days. There were visits to the principal, and letters sent home by post, which, due to some brilliant interception by Boy, never reached its intended recipients. I believe this was the incident that made Boy such a committed atheist for life.

8

Sex

As my favourite sociologist, George Mikes once said, the continentals have sex; the British have the hot water bottle. I do not know if this is true, but young boys in Boy's socio cultural milieu, at least in those days, did not have sex, often did not know about it, or had very dubious notions about it. Boy's situation was no better. And a little understood childhood experience added to the confusion. This is what happened.

Having spent a considerable amount of time in the company of the help, he picked up colourful words and vernacular terminologies for various parts of the anatomy. He learnt that these words elicit furtive giggles and, being soft in the head no doubt, proceeded to repeat them in company. The reaction was not fun. His mother cried, and then reported the matter to his father. His father, with a grim face, enquired about the source of his remarkable general knowledge. The little tattle-tale promptly spilt the beans, and witnessed a scene that shook him.

His normally serious and gentle father suddenly assumed an uncanny resemblance to the demons in his illustrated *Ramayana*. "I will cut you to pieces and bury you here!" he roared at the unfortunate domestic worker. The scene had not been intended for Boy, but as his curious mom was peeping to see, so was he. These transformations of his dad shook him, and it was hard-wired into his brain that the use of certain words had disastrous consequences. As a result, he could not utter profanities in the vernacular ever again.

Years later, during his teen days, this quirk in his character came to be considered the hallmark of a wimp by his fellow adolescents, who expressed their machismo through frequent reference to genitalia, and by punctuating their language with obscenities.

Boy was studying in an eminent Catholic boys' school known for great academic successes and iron discipline. Therefore, Boy was exposed to a collection of highly imaginative and prurient minds. He vaguely followed the smutty discussions, but clearly understood the furtive sniggering.

They were yet to reach puberty, but his cronies seemed to have a vast storehouse of what seemed to him highly improbable facts of life. There was nowhere he could countercheck this information. Books he could access were equally vague on the subject. Asking anyone at home was too outlandish an idea to even occur to him.

Finally a classmate, whose parents were doctors and who, accordingly, claimed authentic information on this taboo subject, smuggled in an elder sibling's biology textbook, revealing the horrific facts about procreation. Boy's reaction was of revulsion, then shock at the idea that even he came into being through such sordid mechanics. But then he consoled himself, "This must be the artificial way that evil people use, and can't be the only way. There must be a good way, where you can perhaps pray for a child, which respectable people like my parents used," he would explain. The junior section had lady teachers, many of them very young and quite pretty. Boy, like most of his classmates, had many crushes and gazed at them with rapt attention. But now, with this horrific knowledge weighing down on his mind, he was racked with guilt, and could hardly look at them without getting warm under the collar. Smutty jokes he had heard earlier and laughed along with everybody without understanding, suddenly became clearer and filled him with revulsion.

Puberty struck, with its army of raging hormones. Revulsion and curiosity battled within him. Boy's school had a 'sister' school, who shared their auditorium. When the young ladies visited his school, the boys were confined to classrooms, caged like wild animals, probably with good justification. The boys hung out of the window and howled like beasts, the only way these hormone crazed frustrated souls could express their admiration. Earlier, Boy had kept himself aloof, feeling disgusted. Nowadays, he would sometimes try to sneak a look.

Finally, Boy went for solutions to the one source that he had complete faith in – books. Ever since learning to read, Boy had been voraciously and indiscriminately devouring anything available in print. But the literature on this taboo subject was not available either at home or the school library, and although his book-for-hire shop had such matter under discreet brown covers, he neither had the money nor the nerve to ask for them.

These books were in circulation amongst the students, and the tattered, crumpled and stained copies were in great demand, especially the ones with pictures. That the language was Scandinavian or Malayalam did not matter, the pictures did. What little Boy could glance at from his furtive peeping over shoulders, disgusted him. This prudery, so uncharacteristic for his age group, remained with him throughout his life. The institution of ragging in college did dilute it considerably, but vestiges of it remained, earning him a reputation as a gentleman among ladies, and a pansy among men.

The print versions he did sample, as he tried every genre of literature without discrimination, but even the immensely popular 'Anonymous,' though rich in imagery, had grammar and style that wounded his sensitive literary soul.

Then he hit pay dirt in his home and school library. The classics had erotic passages; the books that had been removed from the open shelves by his parents when they discovered his appetite for reading, had explosive chapters, and all paid great dividends on patient perusal. Harold Robbins, Samaresh Bose, Kalidasa and Valmiki, all whetted his appetite for erotica.

When elders were impressed by his immersion in the *Ramayana*, he was reading the description of Sita, which would have earned a ban if used in modern literature. Likewise Kalidasa provided titillation with taste, the way poor Anonymous could not dream of.

The only down side was that the relief sought in onanism prostrated him with fear. His misguided teachers during the so called sex education cum moral science class had threatened them with dire consequences, including the inevitable weakness, blindness, loss of sanity and even of life, if they indulged themselves in such "unnatural and sinful" pleasures. Unable to resist, he waited with dread for the just desserts of his crimes.

Fortunately, when I last heard, Boy continued to enjoy reasonable heath and corrected eyesight, and although often considered eccentric, he was not certifiably insane. So Boy, unlike the Englishman, did not have the hot water bottle as a substitute for sex; he had fiction and imagination instead.

9

Light

We had left Boy struggling to make sentences, lost in the labyrinth of the Queen's tongue, and suddenly in the last chapter he is hunting through the classics for salacious passages. The awakening of libido can have extraordinary effects, but not quite to such miraculous levels. A curious reader who is patiently following the saga may be justifiably miffed at this bungling.

Actually it is the fault of Memory, which leaps around through time and space like a performing flea and skipped years at random. We will now try to drag him back and make him fill what gaps he can. It all started with a birthday present in the form of a book, called *The Mystery of the Invisible Thief*. It was written by someone called Gnid Blyton, or so Boy thought. Struggling through it, Boy was completely captivated. Little kids solving crimes that baffled adults, the banter among the children, the yummy sounding food they kept having; in all a new and exciting world opened before his eyes. Solving mysteries through clues where the reader can participate in the problem was wonderful.

He soon exhausted the books by this writer in his class library, which to his disappointment mostly dealt with weird talking toys and similar silly stuff, but Boy's father brought him more from a rental shop, and Boy went through them like a bookworm on steroids. He discovered by now that the writer was a lady called Enid, and had many more stories about other kids and their pets – exciting adventures where the children got into serious trouble but always managed to escape on their own, bringing villains to justice, exploring islands, tunnels, ruins, getting lost, going on picnics and generally having way too much fun. The boarding school stories made him want to go to one.

This also gave him access to other books like *Biggles*, *Billy Bunter*, *Jennings*, *Three Investigators*, *Hardy Boys*, and others of varying merit. Boy wasn't choosy, he devoured all. The racism of Bunter or Biggles or the sexism of Blyton didn't bother him. In fact, he was in love with George, the tomboy.

Boy was in a peculiar situation. He could read English but could not speak it as it wasn't the language at home. He could speak Bangla but couldn't read it. This was the fate of most children in his circumstances. Soon, however, Second Language was introduced in his Anglicised school. He was forced to go through a crash course in Bangla. This opened another magical world of the vast treasure trove of children's and young adult literature available in his mother tongue. Boy's mother, a passionate reader herself, subscribed to all the children's magazines and bequeathed her own childhood library to Boy. Sibram, Sukumar, Tenida and Ghanada became his daily companions. They had a major advantage over the English characters, as they faced familiar circumstances and lived recognisable lives.

The other wonderful source of reading material came from the beautifully illustrated and extremely well written Russian children's literature, as well as folk tales from around the world. In those days, the Indo-Soviet love fest was in full swing. The Marxist government in Bengal had opened stalls all over the city, where, along with dull propaganda, these wonderful children's books were available. Boy's love for these stories and familiarity with Russian names helped him plod through the great Russian novelists when much older. A wag claimed that other than Tolstoy himself and his proof reader, Boy was the only person to have attempted *War and Peace*.

Always a precocious kid, he soon started exploring his parents' libraries. His father had a large collection of English bestsellers, and his mother the latest in Bengali fiction. Boy's father, noting his obsession, had bought him a classics collection and a ten volume encyclopaedia, which kept him engrossed for hours. Thus he was simultaneously reading Blyton and Dickens, Swift, Defoe and Perry Mason, Sukumar, Sibram, Saratchandra and Saradindu. Half understood, often misunderstood, it was just devouring the printed word. It ruined his eyesight, his posture, his social life and his report cards; it basically did what any addiction does. But it opened a window in his life that lit it up and let in a gust of wind that blew out his blues, his fears, his loneliness, and allowed him into fascinating new worlds.

Boy never recovered from this addiction, and paid the price for it, but it helped him recover from other worse addictions that entrapped him while experimenting with consciousness in college. Years later, a senior colleague once warned Boy, "You must not waste your life reading all this rubbish. You are a bright young man. Reading so much dulls the mind, and makes you sluggish." The cunning developed in his youth while hiding other even less socially accepted addictions stood him in good stead now, and he was careful to hide this embarrassing habit of reading from his colleagues. But I have wandered off again, do excuse the digression. Going back to his early youth, in his pre-teens, another lightning struck Boy. He discovered a book called *Something Fresh*. It hooked him from the first passage. It made him snort with laughter and caused major public embarrassment. It was unputdownable.

He discovered a new magical world to escape to. This world was as fantastic as Tolkien's, but much pleasanter. Wodehouse became his chief addiction now. He got thrown out of class for laughing out loud while sneakily reading during lessons. It altered his language and expanded his vocabulary to such an extent that years later, he did not need to struggle through vocabulary enhancement courses to get through competitive examinations, and could ace the language section of CAT without trying. He also discovered erotica. When his parents noticed that he was reading everything on the shelves, they did not apply any bans. Instead, they discreetly removed certain titles from the shelves. Upon noticing this, Boy went on a hunt and found the censored copies nestling inside the clothes cupboard. Intrigued, he investigated and found a treasure trove of forbidden stuff.

The other source of such searing material was hiding in plain sight, in the form of translations from Sanskrit and Persian texts – Omar Khayyam, Kalidasa, Jaydev, Chandidas, and the great epics, Ramayana and Mahabharata. What was more, it was done in exquisite style. Thus it was that his emerging libido helped Boy get a thorough grounding in the classics, as well as earn him a reputation as a devout boy who read religious literature for fun.

This quest for stories took Boy to the next logical step, that of attempting to write some himself. But that we shall save for another day, for the patient and persistent reader.

10

Delhi

D elhi was Boy's accidental love story.

Boy's first visit to Delhi was in his parents' arms, and the only memory that stood out was falling from a high chair in some restaurant. This seems to be the theme of his relationship with Delhi, as he was to return later and fall again into exciting company, a wayward lifestyle, a livelihood, and in love. Like his first fall, it was all by accident.

A holiday with friends to the capital after graduating from school coincided with the college admission season, and informed by his friends that the coolest college in the country was here, he applied to this epitome of snobbery, and was happily selected. Falling in love with the beautiful green campus, with its colonial red brick buildings and rolling lawns dotted by blooming flowers and dazzling damsels, all a sharp contrast to Kolkata's chaotic College Street, he jumped to it. Thus began his lifelong affair with this ancient city, purely by accident.

In college Boy lived out all the clichés. Expanding his horizons, he did not let studies interfere with his education. He opened the 'Doors to Perception,' and being a young under-25 with a heart, became a deep red Communist. Boy fell in love with all the ongoing ideologies, fads and movements that he coincidentally encountered. He also fell in love with a series of young ladies who espoused these causes, but these affairs were largely one-sided. Boy grew out his hair, stopped shaving, dressed in kurtas and flip-flops and joined the "Turn on, tune in, drop out" generation.

Boy also began to discover Delhi. Not just the wide open leafy avenues of Lutyen's Delhi, the international enclaves of Chanakya Puri and Vasant Vihar or the touristy Walled city and the Paratha Wali Gallis, but also the seedy by-lanes of Paharganj, where a very filmy Pathan distributed mind expanding elixirs while a policeman kept watch; the shanty town of Majnu ka Tilla, where the poorest could revel in hooch and offal in the shacks run by Tibetans; the shady doctors in the by lanes around Jumma Masjid who would provide any self-destructive concoction you might crave; the innocuous looking street that sold hardware by day and other wares for the lonely and the depraved at night. And he loved it all. The rich colour of real life, the seedy underbelly of a growing metro; to Boy these were experiences that would help him grow up, develop a soul and become a writer.

But Adam's curse intervened, and the need to earn his daily bhat mach through the sweat of his brow, and Boy left the city for the deep South, to earn his living as a tiny wheel in the vast government machinery. Boy needed a change of scene to heal, for he was suffering his latest heartbreak after yet another wise lady decided that Boy was not the right material for serious relations. Boy did not intend to return, but fate and fatal attraction decided otherwise. He was posted back in Delhi and spent the next decade and a half becoming a native Delhiite, knowing intimately those citizens of Delhi who came there post partition and colonized the city much like the American pioneers. They had the same robust spirit and lived life king-size.

Boy soon became an honorary Punjabi. He also found a Punjaban, who with true Sikh courage decided to risk his company on a long term basis, braving the ire of her community and the communally charged atmosphere which prevailed post the '85 massacres. He finally found love that was reciprocated, once again purely by accident, among dusty ledgers and over a crossword puzzle.

Boy can now do the Bhangra, drink Moga pegs (the elder and stronger brother of the Patiala) in plastic cups with tandoori legs of chicken while parked in a car, and share chutkule in theth Punjabi. Boy has moved out of the city time and again in quest of the daily dal-roti, but returned every time like a boomerang.

This was like an affair that is going to last.

This is the problem with memory. It took him straight from school to adulthood, skipping decades in between. It is rather fond of the fast forward button. But it will be dragged back again, and the patient and persevering reader will see him going to college, getting 'high'er education, and getting married, until he becomes a dad himself, so that he can stop being a boy and finally become a man. Only then can this saga end.

But we shall approach that gradually.

11

College

"It's an IAS-making machine old boy. Put your son in at one end and our pops an IAS at the other." Or so Boy's father's colleague, an old boy, had advised him about the Alma Mater.

As the lone technical imbecile in a family choked solid with engineers for three generations running, the pressure was on Boy to try his luck at the great annual marathon for the Illustrious Avtar Services – as wags call the Indian Administrative Service. He was thus dispatched to the hallowed institution. Situated on what continues to be called the Imperial Avenue, the 'Santon ka Kalij'- as it was described to him by a veteran- was very impressive with its red brick columns and stately lawns. At least to his eyes, accustomed as they were to the crushing crowds of Calcutta.

Boy was eager to make an impression upon the august inmates. Spotting a room with a few lounging figures, he walked in with an outstretched arm and cheery 'Hi.' His beaming smile froze on his lips and he felt as if he had walked into a block of ice. A nerve-racking half an hour later Boy was a wiser man. He learnt that he was a nameless entity called 'fresher.' The lounging dignitaries were 'seniors.' Boy was to address them only as 'Sir,' never sit in their exalted presence, speak only when spoken to, that too without using abbreviations or slang. His time was at their disposal and their wish was his command.

The hostel was called 'Rez,' the room attendant 'GYP' and the canteen 'Cafe' which Boy could not enter except when accompanied by a 'senior.' He had to do odd jobs for these seniors at odd hours and entertain them at all hours. All this was to go on for two months or an intro, whichever was earlier. These rites of passage had been devised to make 'men out of boys' and had the sanction of hoary tradition.

In the process, Boy grew up. The feeling induced by his early academic successes in school – that of being a cat – was reasonably watered down. The last vestiges of self-consciousness, shyness or prudery were brutally extinguished. Chips on shoulders were knocked off, rough edges ground smooth and language altered beyond recognition.

The room was a 'pad,' the bed a 'sack' and sleeping was 'crashing.' K'Nag and K'Bag were Kamala Nagar and Karol Bagh to the uninitiated. C'Sec, CP and GK were easier to follow. A 'fag' was a cigarette or a man of different persuasions- depending on use. 'Zap the chaps' was not a battle cry by captain Spock, but a request for passing the chapattis.

Boy also learnt not to be finicky about food – through a harsh if simple lesson. On the first occasion that he pushed away a barely nibbled at plate, physically ill at the idea of eating this bland and alien tasting fare, an omnipotent Senior stepped in, lectured poor Boy on wastage and bullied him into resuming the meal. Boy was made to finish it, express appreciation and ask for more.

In due course Boy metamorphosed into an omniscient, omnipotent and ominous 'senior' himself. Boy had 'expanded his horizons' and opened 'doors to perception,' doomed to live out clichés. He learnt the import of the old saying, 'St. Stephen was stoned to death and the tradition goes on.'

Huxley, Kerouac, Castaneda, Casey & Ginsberg were his gurus. Boy hotly argued Allende's mistakes and Giap's strategy (for the youth back then followed Vietnamese and South American politics as intensely as youth today follow USA), and discussed Neruda's poetry, Fassbinder's films, neo-existential philosophy and post-Freudian psychoanalysis over endless cups of coffee and charms at the university coffeehouse. He hitchhiked on trucks, or rode borrowed mo'bikes.

Boy read indiscriminately and argued incessantly. He attended Costa Garvas and Ilmaz Gune festivals, lectures by J Krishnamurthy and Mahesh Yogi, theatre workshops by Markus Murch and lec-dems by Amjad Ali and Sonal Mansingh. And, through an exhilarating and tortuous series of true loves, sheer lusts and beautiful relationships, Boy grew up.

The years rolled by and left him beached naked in the cruel world outside the campus cocoon. Boy was a fresher once again- in the real world, this time. It was ragging time all over again, but the 'seniors' this time were sombre men in sober suits. Boy learnt the new ropes and yet another new language of corporate strategies, group motivations and prisoners' dilemmas, and the prize this time round was 'filthy lucre' and graduation to yuppiedom. One thing Boy learnt through all this -growing up is a continuous process.

These memories drift out of a fog, for as a wise man put it, "If you were in Delhi University in the 80s and remember it, you weren't there." Boy was very much there, and remembers little. But how it all started is vivid in his mind. Hang on, that's in Chapter 12.

12

High and Wet

I feel that the idyllic memories of schooldays, the nostalgia for the carefree happy days of school without worry, stress or tension, are largely exaggerated, and probably fueled by alcohol induced amnesia. The horrors of homework, the trauma of tests, the torture of trigonometry, tremors of titration, frustrations of first love- who says school was tension free!

Real freedom was granted in college. Free from the restrictive shackles of home, routine, uniforms, compulsory attendance and unwanted subjects, we were finally free to get an education, without the irksome interference of studies thrown in.

Sadistic school teachers were replaced by laissez faire lecturers, dull uniforms by cool casuals, lunches packed in tiffin boxes by coffee and cutlets in the café, and the opposite sex was in the next seat, not the next school, to be glanced at through barred gates like zoo animals. This, finally, was bliss. Of course, there was a price to pay. After the comforts of home, hostel life was a glimpse into the rigors of real life. The less than hygienic common loos and mass produced bland mess fare was the price of freedom.

Then there was ragging. A rites of passage initiation ceremony harking back to our tribal past, meant to break the ice, forge bonds and make men out of boys. Well, it shattered the ice and all vestiges of diffidence and shyness, and turned you into scarred veterans if you escaped becoming nervous wrecks in the process. The process involved 'interactions' with seniors, entertaining them and doing chores for them.

During one such interaction, Boy was set the task of procuring invigorating libation for the seniors, extracted from malt or molasses. His was not to reason why, so, finances and directions being provided, a very nervous fresher – the tag that newbie initiates went under, Boy left on his quest. In those days, such outlets for liquid refreshment in the capital city were strictly government controlled and few in number, besides having early closing hours. The nearest outlet to the University required changing of buses and, upon arriving at the destination, standing in a long queue with the unwashed multitudes while a policeman kept rioting at bay.

Boy was a sheltered shy youth of 16, thin, bespectacled, with no knowledge of Hindi, the local language. Moreover, he was well below the drinking age, a teetotaler, a law abiding goody-goody fellow just out of school, whose experience of adventure was limited to the pages of the books he was addicted to. Having reached the dispenser of spirits near closing hours after seeking directions in atrocious Hindi from tough looking citizens, causing much mirth, Boy quailed at the prospect of the queue under the stern gaze of the law keepers. But the prospect of meeting his seniors empty handed spurred him on.

He tried to wait with eyes downcast, hiding his face, avoiding the gaze of the policemen and onlookers, among whom he was certain that someone would know his parents and report back his extracurricular activities in college, leading to prompt withdrawal from this brave new world. Ultimately Boy's turn came, and no age related question was raised either by the vendor of spirits or the guardians of the law. The transaction consisted of thrusting a bundle of currency through a grill and shouting, "Do Puri" – Two whole- and two bottles of amber liquid was thrust out of the window. No package, carry bags or anything to disguise the merchandise.

Initial relief at completing his task without jail, exposure, bodily harm or mugging was replaced by the horror of having to carry two exposed bottles back in public transport under the gaze of potential informers or policemen or college authorities or anyone who could ruin his career, character and reputation. The prospect made Boy almost faint with fear. But having spent the money he had no option but to run the gauntlet. Ulysses had it easy he thought, Homer made unnecessary fuss over his journey. Wilting under the stares of the conductor and myriad co-passengers, Boy embarked on the return voyage much like the afore mentioned Ulysses. Imagine the picture, a stripling youth, facial hair yet to appear, grasping two bottles of liquor for dear life, trying hard to look invisible, being jostled in a crowded bus, then creeping along the empty roads of the university, wishing he could melt into the ground.

The final stretch through the college lawns to the hostel was pure purgatory, as Boy imagined every professor's eyes boring into him, with disgrace, expulsion and subsequent interview with his parents flashing before his eyes. Boy reached the sanctuary of the seniors' room without any such mishap and all but collapsed from the stress. The omnipotent seniors then started the rituals of libation after complaining of his tardiness, and as decorum demanded, he was asked, "A drink fresher?" Boy's instinct, indoctrination and intuition demanded he politely refuse, but the memory of what he had undergone to obtain this offering combined with the desperate need for a pick-me-up made him respond- "Yes Sir, thank you," and he proceeded to enjoy the fruit of his expedition.

That was the beginning of Boy's liquid path, and he hasn't looked back since. Other taboos too fell by the wayside during his quest for a degree, which shortly left him High and Dry, but some memories can remain just that, and not even be shared with the reader, at least not yet.

13

Dance

Boy grew up in the East, where leaping about and making a spectacle of yourself was abhorrent to the Bhadralok ethos. He studied in a Catholic boys' school where this vertical expression of horizontal intentions was severely frowned upon. The seventies Kolkata had a happening club life, and Boy had seen older cousins jive to Elvis the pelvis in mixed company, with awe and envy, but was never included in such bacchanals. The only dance the bhadralok were exposed to were ladies in white swaying to Tagore's tunes in his Rabindrik ballets.

Therefore on relocating to the capital, which is an extension of the sunheri sarson ke khet wale pind of the land of five rivers, Boy was taken aback by the tendency of the populace of breaking into a jig at the first opportunity.

Marriage processions had ladies in finery and venerable grandmas jiving in the streets in full view of the hoi polloi, and folk music performances had men in suits prancing around the auditorium, scenes which would give the bhadralok a heart attack. People who danced in streets did so before the Durga idol's immersion procession and constituted solely of the neighbourhood lumpen elements. Of course, much water has flown under the Howrah Bridge since those days, and ladies lead the immersion procession now, dancing with

far greater finesse, and have even crashed the singlet clad male bastion of the Dhunuchi nach, but those days were different.

Recently at a Bhoomi concert, the writer saw the fans of this popular Bangla band, largely middle class bhadralok of both sexes from small towns, dance with vim matching any full blooded Punjabi. A local wag commented that after Chaitanya Mahaprabhu, this is the first time someone made the Bengalis dance.

On relocating to Mumbai the writer discovered that our Gujjubens and Marathi mulgis are no mean twinkle toes themselves, and tend to spice up social events with frenetic twirling. Now Bollywood and Punjabi cultural hegemony has taught the nation to let loose and cut the rug, and even staid Bong weddings have wild dances, and Boy too leaps in and shakes a limb at the slightest opportunity, but in those days the idea was enough to petrify him.

In college Boy came across the institution of the 'Social' where a special dinner and dance were organised and you could invite guests of the opposite sex, and to which the neighbouring girls' college hostellers were also invited en masse.

The idea thrilled him to the core, but on D Day Boy froze, and could not gather enough gumption to ask these strange enchanting beings to partner him for a dance. He watched in agonising envy, his smarter mates inviting these giggling beauties to the floor, and dreading the scurrilous boastings he would have to endure afterwards.

Finally, to induce bravado, Boy decided to fortify himself with the spirit that invigorates, but acquiring it and imbibing it with due secrecy took time, and by the time thus emboldened Boy and his equally shy cronies returned to the venue, the undergrad girls' hostel curfew time was nigh, and the sweet little things were herded back to shelter, protected by the tall walls from hormone charged adolescents. The few ladies left were all graduate students, who seemed like aunties to these just out of school teenagers, and no liquor was strong enough to make Boy approach them for a dance. So Boy leapt about at a distance, imagining that he was dancing with that distant grand dame he could see through a mob of his seniors.

In time Boy too acquired friends of a different gender and won the Holy Grail, an invitation to the girls' college hostel Social. He ventured forth basking in his less fortunate class fellows' envy, but it was a sham. Boy's hostess was from his hometown, a leftist intellectual like the one he professed to be, and spent the time discussing Camus and Kafka while sharing a moody cigarette. They deplored the frivolity of their comrades gyrating lasciviously to throbbing music, while pining away to lose enough inhibition to do the same.

Another year came around. Boy managed to wrangle another invitation from another great buddy in another hostel, who had invited him to hassle her boyfriend. She was an ebullient soul, and insisted on dragging Boy to the dance floor, claiming she had not wasted good money on the guest coupon just to be a wallflower. She promised to teach Boy the moves, and had fortified him with some smuggled spirit to give him Dutch courage, but Boy still couldn't move. Till the band started a cover version of some classic rock and roll, and finally he gave in.

Oh what liberation that was. Flashing strobes, thumping music, bumping bodies, smell of sweat, liquor, cigarettes, perfume and adrenaline, grasping a woman, even a friend's girlfriend, heart racing, hormones raging, it completely blew him to another plane.

Boy hasn't looked back since. However incompetently he does it, he starts leaping around at the sound of any music, and has done the immersion procession dance, the lorry dance, the dhunuchi dance, (remember Devdas? Dola? That's the one.) The bollywood, the disco, the garba, the hip hop, the rap, the waltz, the ragtime, the conga line, even the lungi dance. The dance floor holds no terrors for him. Can't say the same for his hapless partners or fellow revellers, as his skills have not kept pace with his enthusiasm.

But Boy does not care. He could have danced all night…

14

Wild (Part 1)

The tourists spotted some movement in the grass and a flash of colour. Alerted by their excitement, the forest ranger focused his binoculars. To his alarm, he noticed some people hiding in the grass. The tourists' initial disappointment that it wasn't a big cat gave way to renewed excitement at witnessing the capture of some poachers first hand. The ranger sent a wireless message to his colleagues, and soon a posse of guards started giving chase to the unauthorised humans in the tiger reserve.

The interlopers being chased were actually four college kids, having an extraordinary and highly unlawful travel adventure. The fugitives were Ron from Shillong, a crazy guy who was game for anything; Desi from Mumbai, who was the wildlife expert and an extremely law abiding citizen until recently; Jo from Australia who was trying to travel the world on a bicycle; and Boy, the originator of all such harebrained schemes.

It all started a few days earlier in Delhi. Boy and Ron were planning to go backpacking in Goa when Desi wanted to join them, to have an adventure before starting his career in government. He also had some camping gear. So Boy summoned his sleeping bags and backpacks, and promising to show him the real India AND bring him back safely, they took off in the Bombay Mail. Being low on funds, they dispensed with buying tickets and huddled on the floor of the general compartment, where the vast majority of our countrymen travel gratis, being too poor to buy tickets and not much concerned with legalities. Few ticket checkers brave those crowds to catch offenders.

On the way, Desi spoke of the Ranthambore tiger reserve, which he hadn't been to, and which was not far from Sawai Madhopur, a station they were passing through. So a toss of a coin decided that they get off there, and continue their journey after a detour to this forest. From Sawai Madhopur, they hitched a lift on a tractor up to the village at Ranthambore. While waiting for a lift, Boy met Jo and his bicycle, with a fund of stories of cycling around the heart of India. Fascinated, he promptly co-opted him into their team, and dragged him along.

Utter disappointment awaited them at Ranthambore. There was no budget accommodation, and to enter the forest they needed a permit, only available at Sawai Madhopur. Dejected, Boy decided to explore the ancient ruins and temple in the nearby hill and look for some food and shelter in the tiny hamlet there.

Here the warm embrace of Bharat awaited Boy... Not knowing the dialect, and Desi being the only one with passable Hindi, they mimicked eating and sleeping to the ladies in all-encompassing ghunghat, who seemed to be the only people there. They were invited into one of the homes, and fed what seemed like large lumps of roasted dough with ghee along with tall brass tumblers of buttermilk. This was Boy's first introduction to the famed Dal Bati and Chach. The giggling ladies whose faces remained firmly behind veils found everything about them extremely amusing – their lack of appetite when they couldn't consume the mountains of food offered, not knowing the language, seeking shelter at the village, and their desire to explore the forest on foot. Falling over each other in laughter, they laid some charpoys in their courtyard and directed them to take a siesta, which they gratefully accepted.

Refreshed, they explored the ruins and visited the ancient temple, where a Rana was said to have offered his own head as a sacrifice to Shiva and been suitably rewarded. They bathed and swam in the ancient tank by the temple, then got scared off by the resident turtles, which they took to be crocodiles, since they'd seen plenty basking by the lake.

In the evening the men folk returned, and over communal chillums they promised to take the group along with them to the forest the next day, when they went to graze their cattle and collect firewood and other forest produce – illegally, but what the law denied them, tradition had promised. Thrilled, Boy thanked them, and politely declining further hospitality, they went to sleep in the ruins with many warnings from their hosts to never let the fire go out at night, or else…

So they decided to take turns to stay up and tend the fire, eating bajre ka rotis and achar and gur which the villagers had packed for them. They made tea in Jo's billycan, without which all Australians are incomplete, and after sharing a companionable chillum, slept off in the deep silent forest among the ancient ruins where people offered heads to Gods. Jo's cycle was left in the village.

Boy was woken up early in the morning by their hosts and strongly admonished, for they were all sleeping soundly and the fire was off. This was good, for they could at most have been eaten by passing predators, but an untended fire could have caused a forest fire and done untold damage. Duly chastened, Boy meekly followed them into the core area.

After a thrilling trek where every bush seemed to hide lurking beasts, but spotting nothing more ominous than herds of cheetal and neelgai, packs of langoors and numerous birds, especially peacocks, they were escorted to a cave, said to be occupied by a sadhu, the sole human resident of the forest, who was to be their host that night. The villagers shared a meal and the communal chillum with them and left rations of chana and gur, telling them not to stray and to stay out of sight, away from tourist jeep routes, animal paths and forest guards, who in their view were more to be feared than the resident tigers. They were also shown the escape route in case they were spotted, as the guards had no jurisdiction outside the boundaries, and the nearest police station was in Sawai Madhopur. Boy's offer of monetary compensation was turned down with hurt pride. He apologized and parted friends. They bathed in the stream by the cave and settled down in the coming dusk, waiting for the Sadhu in his cave while listening to the myriad forest sounds.

He came in silently, unsurprised by strangers in his abode, and taught Boy how to make rotis on bare rock among small flames and curry from some wild roots and berries. He taught them the right way to fill, light and smoke a chillum. He spoke of his life and the reasons for this solitary life, his philosophy, the forest, and living in harmony. But that will be another story.

Thus started the second night in the forest, deep inside, but not pitch dark, as stars twinkled and moonlight filtered in through the trees, and not silent either, as the forest sounds from the stream, wind, trees and unseen creatures filled the night. The herbal stimuli were making Boy's mind see animals at every shadow, and the unaccustomed diet was making his stomach rumble. Fear prevented Boy from moving out to the bushes to relieve the rumblings, and his companions prevented him from polluting the environment near the cave.

As to how this was resolved, and further encounters with wild animals and wilder guards, and how they survived to tell the tale, will come in episode two.

15

Wild (Part 2)

We left our hero, i.e. Boy, in a dilemma. This was resolved, quite literally, by a cliff-hanger. Boy hung over the cliff outside the cave, clutching at vines for dear life, praying the tiger wasn't about to pounce, and got rid of the excess Rajasthani hospitality that his delicate Bong system was loathe to accept. Early next morning, woken not by birdcalls but by screeching langoors, they climbed down to the stream for a morning frolic, unaware of the import of the langoors' agitation. Soon the frantically gesticulating Sadhu called them back to the cave. There, he gently chided Boy for destroying the harmony of the forest. Apparently, the stream was part of the beat of a tigress, and the langoors were announcing the presence of her majesty. Unknown to the city folk but evident to the Sadhu, she had made a kill last night, had enjoyed the meal at her favourite spot a short stroll away, and had been coming down to the pool for a refreshing drink when their rude transgressions disturbed her majesty. The Queen of the forest had left in a huff, and withdrawn into deeper forest.

After a breakfast of Roti and Aloo courtesy the forest hermit, and tea courtesy Jo and his billycan, and after enjoying the morning chillum and satsang, their host showed Boy the way to the lake via the stream, with a warning not to disturb the kill. Slightly sceptical, giving credit to the hallucinatory qualities of good jungle weed,

they rounded the bend and stood still in shock! There, on a flat rock just below the overhang lay the gory remains of a Sambar. Boy did not disturb the kill. It was the kill that deeply disturbed him. The pugmarks leaving the stream were clearly visible in the sand. They seemed very fresh. The thought that this kill could have been them anytime that they were walking around this area, when Boy was relieving himself late last night, or taking a dip this morning, all the times they were within sniffing distance of this mayhem, made their hair stand on end. Boy hurried down the path, cursing Desi for having got them into this.

Further shock awaited Boy, but a beautiful one this time. In the tall grass, he came face to face with a majestic Sambar stag. They both froze for seconds, gazes interlocked, when suddenly someone let out a breath and the magic was broken. The stag disappeared with a mighty leap. The four reached the ruins by the lake and found shelter, where they carefully lit a fire since the tourist lodge was on the opposite bank and they had to stay hidden. They dined on the villagers' gur and chana and Jo's porridge and settled down, taking turns to mind the fire and stand guard. Jo had been carrying a Lonely Planet guide, but blown away by this experience which no guide book could have prepared him for, he decided to donate the pages to rolling Js.

After an incident free night they rose at dawn with the light shimmering on the lake and water birds everywhere. Herds of cheetal were at the lake, oblivious of them. As the sun rose, they saw some crocodiles sunning themselves on the bank. This led to a problem as their water was being rationed for drinking only and they needed more for washing and for tea. They drew straws and Boy lost. With the billycan, a jerry can and a stick, he went down quaking, stomping to make the crocs leave, as advised. They slithered off into the water. But the water near the edges was murky and covered in green scum, making it opaque. He was certain the prehistoric beasts were lurking just under, waiting to drag him down. Ignoring his friends' encouragements to go in and get clean water, Boy stood safely on the bank, as far from the water as possible. He hooked the billycan and jar on the stick and collected muddy water full of flotsam and vegetation. Jo patiently strained it through a cloth, boiled it and made tea, tricks he had learnt in the Great Australian Outback, and everyone had tea and porridge and left to explore the lake.

Finally their luck ran out. Some tourists mistook them for tigers, and disappointed on finding some kids instead, alerted the guards, and that's where the story took off in Part 1. Hearing the commotion and realizing that they were exposed, Boy and his friends stopped hiding in the grass, where they had crouched upon the jeeps' approach, and made a run for the fence, which was quite close by there. Boy leapt to the tree their village friends had pointed out, whose branches straddled the fence, and throwing their rucksacks over, they all climbed the tree and jumped the fence. The guards were still some hundred yards away.

Boy' great escape was being avidly watched by a college bus trip waiting on the road outside. Boy whetted their curiosity while Jo hurriedly collected his cycle from the villagers, whom they profusely thanked in broken Hindi. Then the students gave them a lift to Sawai Madhopur, providing a meal and transportation in exchange for their stories, much like the troubadours of old.

They decided to dispense with buying tickets again, much to Jo's delight, and decided to spend their remaining funds on a local brew called Santara. This was too potent for poor Desi, a teetotaler till then, but after the recent strain on the nerves he decided to sample some, and promptly passed out. The first Delhi bound train that arrived was jam packed, and they just managed to get a foothold in a doorway by pleading an ill companion and showing the prone Desi. So space was made, the poor in our country being compassionate people, and Desi was stuffed between people's feet, while Boy sat on the steps of the open doorway. Jo used his skin colour to store his cycle in a first class compartment and came to join Boy. They spent the night perched on the moving train's steps, occasionally pulling the comatose Desi out so that he could be sick on the tracks. They reached Delhi alive and returned to their hostel and Jo to his backpackers' dorm.

Boy returned to find an appointment letter waiting, and has been serving that sentence since. Desi went on to top the Civils, and is a glamorous diplomat now. Ron lived out his dreams, travelled the world, running canteens, gambling dens, being a tea taster despite drinking only alcohol, and is now settled in Europe. Jo, after a short stay in Delhi, cycled off into the sunset, never to be heard from since. Boy did not get to see the tiger on that trip, though he would see many much later. But for all of them, this was one incredible, wild, illegal, dangerous trip that they never should have undertaken, but are glad they did, because this experience can never be repeated or forgotten.

This trip obviously had no photographic evidence other than those seared in their minds.

16

Work

The patient reader who has been following the story may have wondered how the delinquent ended up employed in a respectable profession. Here is the story. It was all thanks to the college Don, the gang lord kind that is, not the academic – Bhai.

Boy met Bhai in the Government Hostel, which housed students across disciplines from the University. Seats were allotted per course or institution, based on merit, with the usual reservations for various sectors. The actual number of students staying illegally far exceeded the allotted seats. Boy was always good at MCQ tests that did not require in depth domain knowledge. Tests of reasoning came easily to him, and verbal skills were taken care of by his obsession with Wodehouse. Thus having scored very well in the university admission tests, he secured a prized hostel seat, promptly collected illegal guests who matched his bohemian lifestyle, and settled in.

Here he met an interesting selection of students from diverse backgrounds. In his earlier elite college, there were kids from all over the country and abroad, but who all fell into the same broad socio-economic and cultural grouping of elitist anglicised achievers. Here, he was attracted to the groups who were completely alien to his experience.

Bhai was from the heartland and looked down upon the effete products of the 'Santo ki Kalij,' as he termed Boy's Alma Mater, and bullied them for entertainment. But the brotherhood of the inebriated soon melted barriers, and the Don, impressed that there could be regular guys from such rarefied institutions, took Boy under his wing and decided to teach him about the real world.

This included spoken Hindi, abuses in various dialects, how to steal petrol from bikes, "borrow" random bikes or even cars, sell cinema tickets on the black-market, eat for free in restaurants, watch films for free, procure tickets for sold-out shows, browbeat timid looking people, relieve rich kids of excess cash by involving them in card games, acquire all types of goods and services which the law of the land had prohibited, and more – basically the skill set necessary for urban survival.

Boy had taken a summer job where he had to convert answers to questionnaires into binary cards for a market research firm. He took it to be in an air-conditioned environment to beat the Delhi summer, meet girls and earn some pocket money.

Bhai came to investigate where his protégé was disappearing every day, and understanding how the system worked, immediately hatched a money making plan. On his instructions, Boy struck a deal with his employers. After ascertaining what they expected as a good day's work, he offered to take up a contract for a week's work for ten students, to be delivered the next day. Intrigued, the boss agreed to the scheme. They then proceeded to take the workload to the hostel, where the Don's henchmen rounded up dozens of unfortunate freshmen undergoing their "initiation," and promptly put them to work translating the data into the cards, with the stipulation that it must be completed overnight.

The boss was thrilled to see such instant results. Boy and Bhai organised a major bacchanal with the resultant bonanza. Thus the idea of outsourcing with slave labour was born.

Bhai ensured that Boy passed his exams despite not attending any classes, by extorting the notes of the diligent students for him with the use of innovative threats, and even organised special night-long coaching for him under these same unfortunate students on the nights before the exams. He also provided the pharmaceutical help to stay up through the nights and the subsequent examination days. The major pastime of Delhi University students is preparing for the marathon Civil Service Examinations. The first part was MCQ, which along with general IQ and verbal knowledge, tested one subject and General Knowledge as well. Boy's habit of indiscriminate reading had his GK quite up to par, and his concepts on the subject he was supposed to be studying were quite clear, plus his penchant for MCQs ensured that he could clear this round without having to get sober. But the second round of detailed domain knowledge was beyond him, having practically dropped out of college by then.

Bhai was very impressed with Boy's MCQ test clearing abilities. He had seen Boy clear the dreaded CAT exams earlier while barely sober. Bhai had hijacked a blazer, coaxed him into a haircut and shave, and sent him for the interview for the prestigious management institutes. But the blazer wasn't enough to counter Boy's Marxist ranting during the interview, and he was laughed out of a place, much to his relief, by the board.

Bhai now provided a solution. "Look, we are from the middle class, and will soon need to have some job to earn a living. Corporate sector won't hire you if you talk such rubbish. Our parents think that we will be Civil Servants. But we should know our limitations. We can never get around to working hard enough to make it. During the first attempt, we will be fussed over at home, as a future IAS. During the second, they would have cooled off. During the third, they will throw the roti at us… Let us try for the Public Sector companies instead. You can get jobs there by marking ticks on the paper. And they won't mind your dress sense or crazy ideas. All these studious classmates will join the same companies after failing the Civils thrice. We will be their bosses and rag them then."

Plan finalized, Bhai proceeded to keep track when vacancies were declared, as Boy was too lazy to care; pay for Boy's forms, as he was too broke to buy them himself; fill them for him, as he was too laid-back to do so; wake him up on the exam mornings, and even drop him to the exam centres on "borrowed" bikes.

Boy duly cleared the exams. His kindly interviewers gently chided him and told him what not to say in interviews, but proceeded to select him anyway. Boy chose the job with the earliest joining date, and continues there till today. Bhai's prediction turned out to be accurate, and many contemporaries, after unsuccessful attempts at the IAS, joined his company later as his juniors.

Bhai himself is leading a quiet life in some backwaters, after his colourful and mercurial career suffered a setback due to some change in political fortunes. Boy gratefully acknowledges his debt to this unlikely coach, a college don, for getting him thus respectably employed.

17

Limelight

We have seen Boy start life as a reclusive bookworm and a shrinking violet, in dread of the limelight, shunning it with passion and cunning, preferring anonymity. People who knew him then wondered how on earth he summoned up enough nerve to propose to a real live girl and get her to agree. He was one of nature's wallflowers. Gussie Fink-Nottle could have taken a correspondence course from him.

People who know him now cannot believe this ever was so. Shun it?! He revels in it! He loves his fifteen minutes of fame that every 21st century citizen is entitled to in these times of media madness. He loves to hog the limelight. These days Boy is upset if he is not the life and soul of the party. When he gets the mike on the podium, he is reluctant to let go. He is the idiot who asks the long question at the seminar just to get the mike and the spotlight, when everyone is desperate to rush at the cocktails.

Boy does not mind the spotlight for the wrong reasons either, like when performance awards are being announced the morning after a boisterous night during the review meetings, and the spotlight finds the awardees, like Boy, fast asleep, and the picture on the screen gets vociferous cheers. But this was not always the case. He used to be the good boy who was seen and not heard while in school, as the loyal reader has seen earlier. He died many deaths when up on stage for a debate or a minor role in a play. Even in birthday parties while playing passing the parcel, he would want to sink through the carpet when the pillow stopped with him and he was made to stand up and recite something. This fear made Boy avoid parties and school events. Being a thin dark bespectacled bookworm didn't quite add to his social confidence. His only skill was the ability to make wisecracks, often at others' expense, and this was his defence mechanism. Then how did it all change?

In one word – ragging. The much reviled institution which is supposed to break sensitive souls actually made Boy break out of his shell.

When he discovered that the only way to avoid doing chores for seniors in the hostels was to entertain them; a stand-up comic was born. He literally told jokes for survival, like the hero of the celebrated Roald Dahl story forced to keep making a gangster laugh in order to be left alive; and soon the heady sound of laughter and the social acceptance that followed became like a drug. And he could get away with insulting the bullies under the guise of humour. What a powerful weapon to have.

But the final shreds of shyness were surgically removed in the cinema halls. The 'freshers' or first year students, the poor victims of the great institution of ragging, were taken to shows by seniors who even paid for their tickets (in the front stalls of course), but there was a price to pay.

During the innumerable songs that slowed the plot, Boy and his fellow sufferers were made to climb the podium in front of the screen and perform the dances along with the heroine and her backup chawannis and duanis, mimicking their gyrations, to the accompanying whistles, catcalls and thrown peanuts from the hoi polloi who frequented these theatres.

Once you have gyrated your hips in sync with Rekha or Helen to general applause from the lungi clad hard nuts of North Delhi, no stage can faze you ever again.

18

Free lunch

B oy, having read *Ten Days that Shook the World* and seen the film *Reds*, where John Reed is played brilliantly by Warren Beatty, had become a fan. Emulating the hero, he put up the sign on his hostel room – 'Property is Theft! Walk in' – and left the door unlocked. His friends pointed out that as he had no property, his visitors would more likely take pity on his impoverished state and leave something behind. But it was the principle that mattered.

He however attracted uninvited guests, the jetsam of the last of the flower children who were still around in the Eighties, and who drifted in and out of Boy's room. One day, on his return from Diwali break, Boy found a strange bearded man of uncertain nationality sleeping in his bed. Enquiry revealed that the hostel chowkidars had discovered the man passed out in the lawns, and assuming him to be Boy's guest, had kindly shifted him to the room. This strange guest stayed on a few days, and disappeared equally suddenly.

Boy also learnt to consider all property as communally owned, and happily borrowed items of clothing, furniture and transportation from hapless co-residents. This was all in line with the principle of 'to each according to his needs.' Old Marx had a capital idea!

His permanent guest was Ron, Boy's friend and life coach, who, unknown to the University authorities, shared Boy's room throughout his stay. The loyal reader will remember him from the previous escapades, notably the stint in the Ranthambore forests.

Among Ron's many accomplishments was his skill at being an uninvited guest at every wedding or function in the vicinity. He generously imparted this knowhow to his many admirers. The trick was to borrow blazers or suits from their sartorially natty brethren, and confidently walk into the party. For weddings the best time was just after the 'baraat' or groom's party went in.

Ron's method was to survey the area, zero in on the most promising party, and invite himself in. Ron even asked after the health of 'Pappu,' a ubiquitous Punjabi name, and the host would often issue instructions for special care to be taken of them as Pappu's friends. I understand that functions in that area budgeted for an extra five percent for such uninvited guests. Even when suspected, no one wanted to create a scene, and Boy and his friends survived on benefit of doubt, the innate decency of their unknowing hosts, and sheer chutzpah.

Ron's height of cool was on display when they were politely escorted out of one party where they had been unfortunately unmasked. On being politely asked by the hosts about his identity, Ron had guilelessly confessed to being an uninvited student, but was careful enough to give wrong college particulars. After being escorted out, he calmly strolled into yet another party the same night to resume his meal, insisting that he had not yet had his dessert.

Their crowning glory was gate crashing an international convention at a five star venue, which went off successfully once Boy dissuaded Ron from hijacking the stage. On that occasion, having sneaked into a party at a five star hotel, they discovered that it was an international symposium on labour relations. Ron promptly assumed the persona of a Greek delegate, and advised Boy to play the Bangladeshi representative. After partaking liberally of the wines available, Ron decided he had to make a speech to thank the hosts. Only upon Boy's ceaseless persuasion that such a speech would make detection inevitable, and criminal prosecution followed by expulsion from college would logically follow, was the plan abandoned, and they left the venue waving amicably at the puzzled hosts.

The biggest disaster Boy faced was when, on sneaking into a gala event, he noticed an alarming number of his professors amongst those present. He beat a hasty retreat, congratulating himself on his narrow escape. But fate had decided otherwise. A couple of years later, when Boy was a respectable government official, going steady with a very decorous lady, and his scandalous history a deeply veiled secret, it decided to strike!

Delhi had been savaged by communal strife, and Boy was working with a relief team. Loyal readers have read of his experiences in this traumatic and shameful black spot in our history in an earlier chapter. Boy noticed that his team leader was a senior professor from the University. Boy introduced himself as his one time student, who unfortunately had not met him owing to not having attended any classes, being a misguided youth, when the renowned professor cut in, "Of course I know you!

You are the guy who gatecrashed our Dean's daughter's wedding!" The super hit film *Three Idiots* not having glamourised this activity at that time, Boy shrank under the shocked gaze of his fellow relief workers.

A word of warning dear friends, our disreputable past has a nasty habit of catching up with us when least expected, no matter how deep you bury it. It is best to have a blameless history. But then again, who wants a boring past.

19

Cops

The sight of policemen gave Boy the heebie-jeebies. Whether it was due to some deep rooted phobia of the tools of colonial oppression based on subconscious racial memory, or merely a guilty conscience, we cannot say. For laws are myriad and the intent of compliance not so robust, leading to occasionally catching the eye of her keepers.

It was during his impecunious student days that Boy, whenever he couldn't persuade kindly strangers to offer lifts, travelled the city and even the country using public transport, but neglected the formality of coughing up the fare. Sometimes the keepers looked askance at these liberties, and ingenuous ruses would keep Boy from their clutches. A classic save was orchestrated by his friend Boss, who later went on to become a major scourge for lawbreakers himself.

The bus had been stopped for a spot check just outside the hostel, so Boss decided impromptu to jump off and run, with the checkers in hot pursuit. Boy and his gang slipped quietly into the hostel while the law, in the form of a puffing constable, was diverted by Boss.

"Show us your ticket," the official demanded, upon finally catching hold of the fugitive a few roads down.

"Don't have any"

"Then come to the police station!"

"I won't"

"We can make you!"

"No you can't, I have a Pass," and Boss flourished his monthly bus pass.

"Then why did you run?" asked the flummoxed arm of law.

"Is running against the law?" came the prompt reply, related later to gales of laughter at the hostel.

Today, as a consultant, Boss provides similar loopholes to his clients.

On another occasion, the law keepers wanted ID to prove that Boy and his friends had reached the legal age for the activity they proposed. Boss gravely informed them that simple living and Yoga keeps them looking young, for if they had been married off by their parents at an appropriate age, they would have children as old as those guardians of the law. Rolling with laughter, they very kindly let Boy and his cronies proceed.

Boy was also reluctant to pay the necessary fees to attend shows and exhibitions, and always knew of an unguarded back entrance, convenient low wall or break in the fence. Neither did Boy wait for invitations to attend parties, receptions, and weddings hosted by complete strangers. This too led to occasional detection and disagreements, and a host of aliases had to be kept handy when made to provide names and addresses.

The other occasions for incurring the displeasure of the law had moral right on Boy's side, or so he believed, as it was for creating disruptions for various dimly understood causes, in the name of student protest. The Police were unusually patient and polite with students, and arrested them merely to let them go a few hours later, dutifully noting down the names, and not expressing any surprise that they were all named after the Prime Minister of the country.

But once things went out of hand and a group was taken to the lockup overnight, with some talk of fingerprinting the next day. A number of the inmates had interviews to attend in the near future, and many were aspiring civil servants whose careers would crash-land if weighed down by police records. As they were held in a temporary camp in a school building, it was a simple matter to escape through the windows, and many did.

Trouble brewed the next day, when everyone was being let off post negotiations, and the head count did not tally. If the same number of students weren't released, the cops could be charged with Habeas Corpus. An ingenious solution was found. Certain students, including Boy and Ron, broke INTO the lockup, with full police cooperation, to make up the numbers originally picked up. They were then immediately released to fanfare from the student leaders.

Although student agitations were a friendly match with the cops, post-exam high jinks were sometimes frowned upon. On one such spirited occasion, on a whim and a dare, a few of them, including Boy and Ron, decided to climb a statue of a national hero adorning the town square. This attracted a crowd, and soon a uniformed friend with a large stick.

Boy naturally did not heed the cop's injunctions to descend at once, but instead climbed higher to escape the flailing stick. The intrepid law keeper then decided to climb after them, forcing Boy to take drastic measures before backup arrived. They accordingly leapt to the ground in different directions and fled for their lives, guessing that the cop could chase only one of them. They escaped, cheered on by the watching crowd and helped along by onlookers always siding with the wrong side of the law.

Boy has since grown up into a law abiding citizen, and some of his friends have become law makers and keepers themselves, where the worst crimes they commit are minor traffic violations. But even now, confrontations do happen.

Getting late for work, Boy once tried speeding through as the lights were changing, and was promptly stopped by a lurking guardian of the law. He tried to plead that they were on the same side, both being government servants on official duty, and after scrutinising his credentials the policeman claimed that Boy was only partly government. Boy pointed out that he had only partly jumped the light. Impressed by this astute argument, he waved Boy on with a broad grin on his face.

20

Girls

Boy developed many passions as he grew up to top up his addiction to reading, which he had developed early in life. He became interested in cinema, music, theatre, travel and poetry, and became involved with social work and adventure sports. The thin finicky boy even grew into a keen foodie.

But the one passion that led to all the rest was the one that he shared with the entire male heterosexual adolescent population – GIRLS!

It is said that around the time one enters the teens all boys are afflicted with two infestations, but Bong boys are inflicted with three. Whilst everyone finds a dark smudge discolouring their upper lip and the sudden transformation of every female human not closely related by blood into this mesmeric being, Bong kids have the additional burden of poetry bubbling within them. All three are inevitable and equally irresistible. Boy was no exception.

Being a thin dark lanky bespectacled bookworm, Boy's interest in the fairer species was not reciprocated, and his confidence in making an approach run was near absolute zero, that is, minus 273 degrees. His being in a boys' school did not help matters.

Then one day, a miracle occurred. Deeply uncomfortable in mixed company as always, Boy reverted to his standard defence mechanism, making wisecracks. He heard some feminine giggles amongst the usual sniggers and was mortified. Nature, in her generosity in providing him with melanin, had made it impossible for him to blush, but he grew hot under the collar.

This was routine for him. But suddenly, looking up, he noticed that those pretty eyes were not looking at him with derision, but with interest! He tentatively tried cracking a few more jokes, and was thrilled to notice that the young ladies were not laughing at him, but at his jokes. This transformed him. He became the insufferable class joker. His caustic wit and sarcasm kept him within perilous proximity of a sound thrashing by his more robust classmates, and got him sent out of class regularly by irate teachers.

He also discovered that certain young ladies were more impressed by his vast storehouse of irrelevant trivia, a by-product of his voracious reading. (Reader, remember that was the pre-Google era, where information wasn't a tap away.) And those certain young ladies also read books and enjoyed talking about them. His life was made.

Boy had a major complex about his unflattering looks, and despite his great enthusiasm, about his very modest success as an athlete. That is why he tried extra hard to impress with whatever meagre talents he did possess.

He discovered that a striking young lady was a ghazal and thumri aficionado, and pretended to be one too. Though he couldn't sing, he could at least listen and admire. Soon, he developed a genuine keen interest in this genre.

Similarly, he discovered that SPICMACAY, the society promoting classical music and arts, was patronised largely by young ladies, and that the jocks steered well clear of it. He promptly joined, and suffered many long evenings with the Dagar brothers droning on, or some Diva dancing, or the caterwauling of some strange instrument until it all began to make sense, and enthral him.

With equally dubious motives he trailed along to art galleries staring incomprehensibly at weird squiggles, and slept through a screening of (aesthetes, please don't die of shock) Fellini's *Eight and a Half* in the company of intellectual ladies. But it paid rich dividends. Today he loves world cinema, and collects prints of Indian masters.

But it was not only wimpy arty stuff that that he got into in his single-minded pursuit of beauty. He went trekking with the short haired sporty kinds and developed a lifelong love for the outdoors. He went to all-night Rock concerts with the chain-smoking spiky haired beauties, only to become a devotee of Jim Morrison, Bob Marley, and the Man from Tennessee.

His very brief foray into martial arts was not inspired by Bruce Lee like the rest of his generation, but a comely young lass who gave coaching. Like all the other ladies of various talents, this coach too was oblivious of his passion, but Boy developed an unfounded confidence which helped him face up to roughnecks in his later delinquent youth.

Poetry was the one art which beat him, and still does, though he faked it then and fakes it now, as there is no greater magnet for the soulful lady than poetry. In his early teens he would spout heartfelt poetry and write some too, quite sincerely, for his then current crush. Thankfully those that tendency has since disappeared. You can blame that on his Bong genes.

As you can see, Boy did not discriminate. As long as she was female, and would tolerate his company, Boy would happily tag along. But unfortunately the reverse wasn't true. Although these ladies tolerated Boy's company for the entertainment value in short spells, they soon moved on. But in their wake, they left Boy enriched with new interests and passions.

Did Boy die a bachelor then? No, dear reader, and a little more patience will tell you the how and the why. It's just a couple of chapters away.

21

Pets

B oy has come to believe that true love is the K9 kind.
His first canine love was his grandfather's Dachshund
Bhulo, sleek, black and short, who would let him cuddle her,
which he did whenever they visited. She had a keen musical
ear, and would join in with mournful howls whenever
anyone sang, whether in protest or appreciation Boy was not
quite clear. He was a toddler then, and professed his desire to
marry her when older. Boy also remembers crying copiously
when he heard of her demise. His next was a communally
owned mongrel called Jimmy, whom Boy called Makua and
fed his school lunch in exchange for being licked all over. But
she wasn't allowed indoors. But the first dog of Boy's very
own was Kumkum, a Fox Terrier – Pomeranian cross, whom
he picked up from his cousin and hand reared with milk fed
through eye drop dispensers.

Having been trained by Boy, the poor creature grew up
thoroughly confused, but with an uncanny human cunning.
For example, she was prohibited from sleeping on the bed
and obediently slept in her basket till Boy's mother had
bid him goodnight. The moment her footsteps died away
however, Kumkum would promptly leap onto the bed and
snuggle under the covers. She was equally quick to return to
her basket just before mom came to wake Boy up.

They were partners in crime. Boy used to be locked up in a room with his books when exams approached, and she would keep him company. The couch being banned to her, she would peacefully curl up on the rug till the door was locked. Moments later she would spring up on the sofa, and the book in Boy's hands would immediately be switched to something more readable. And when mom came back to check, the alert canine ears picked up the footsteps well in time, and the switch happened before the door opened. Kumkum would be back on the floor, and the textbook back in Boy's hands.

She was also a sneak thief. Convinced that what Boy ate at the table was way better than what was served in her dish, she would not be content to merely beg for scraps with melting eyes, in which endeavour she was extremely successful, but also sneak off some tasty tit bit from the plate if it was left unwatched for a moment. Her post-crime strategy was always to go into hiding, so whenever she wasn't underfoot, Boy knew some rule had been broken.

Kumkum knew very well who mattered at home, and gave no attention to any commands from anyone except mother. To get her to do your bidding, all one had to say was "Ma ke dakbo" (I'm going to call mother). An essentially Bengali dog, she also loved her fish and rice, sweets, luchi, muri, singara or samosa and would not touch dog food.

She understood idiomatic Bengali and through subtle variations in her barks, whines and growls, managed to convey a wealth of meaning. She loved to join in Boy's games, fielding expertly in cricket, except that being a free spirit she wouldn't follow the rules and made up her own. This usually involved the whole team chasing her to retrieve the ball.

Cricket balls survived the ordeal with some loss of shine, but tennis balls and badminton shuttles did not usually survive her intervention.

Being a product of Boy's training school, the idea of discipline was totally alien to her.

Boy left for college, and the move to a new city and an exciting independent life kept him engrossed enough not to miss her. On his return home for vacations, he discovered what he had missed.

Even before Boy reached the door, a major commotion broke out. Her joy was expressed in dashing around the house, upsetting furniture, leaping up on Boy and knocking off his glasses. Her welcoming barks alerted the neighbourhood that something special was happening, making it amply evident that here was someone who really missed Boy, and was glad to see him back.

She was a jealous dog, and when Boy returned home some years later with a new bride, made it clear that not everyone was happy with this development. Whenever Boy and his new bride sat next to each other, she would promptly get in between them and slyly show her teeth to Boy's wife. By now Kumkum was a senior citizen, and her right to the couch was well established.

Over time and many visits home, the two loves of Boy's life learnt to tolerate and even grow quite fond of each other. A few years later, at the ripe old age of 15, a much mellowed Kumkum died fighting cancer in a post-surgery relapse, and was cremated in a quiet animal crematorium. Her timing was perfect, she waited till all three brothers (Boy's siblings whom we have kept strictly under wraps) were home together, something that rarely happened any more.

After Kumkum, Boy swore not to keep a dog again, and not expose himself to this trauma. But when his brother turned up with a tiny Doberman pup, the resolve wavered, and Police came home to guard them when she grew up.

Trained by an official trainer of police dogs, Police (or Pulu for short) grew to be a complete terror, with loyalty only to Boy's dad, tolerating the rest of them only for his sake.

Visitors to Boy's family home dwindled, his father's bridge playing group met elsewhere. No one came home to deliver groceries, pick up the laundry, read the meters or solicit for charity.

But she held no terror for Boy's two kids, one just a toddler, and Police patiently bore with their exuberant affections. It must have chaffed her proud spirit to be pulled by the ear by a child, ignoring her rumbling growls, and she took it out on the next hapless visitor to our compound – two legged or four. With old age, she began to refuse food if Boy's father wasn't around, and he grew increasingly homebound. Boy's mother then had to sometimes visit her sons in different continents alone. Police celebrated her absence by laying claim on the bed, and sleeping with her head on mom's pillow.

The worst part of having a K9 love is that we have vastly different life spans. A much mellowed Police, 14 winters down, could hardly see, eat or walk, but still her reputation was enough to keep the home and gardens free from trespassers, visitors and even cats. When the vet gave up hope, dad refused to put her down or send her to the hospital where she would miss the family. She survived on saline and intravenous drips for three days, till Boy's brothers arrived from their respective places in the world, and buried her in the garden. Boy's father decreed there would be no more dogs in the family.

Not long after, Boy's father too left to join his favourite companion, and was not around to impose his decree. Boy succumbed to his children's entreaties, and a black lab puppy came home. The condition was, that all poop cleaning, puppy sitting, walks, wash, feed, training and housebreaking were exclusively to be the kids' department.

Kola, as she was christened, short for Boka Kola (a misnomer, as she proved humanly intelligent), was of an angelic temperament. Trained with military precision by Boy's daughter, she was as obedient as no dogs he had seen outside of the cinema. She wouldn't eat from the floor or drink from the toilet, there being no question of begging at the table leave alone stealing food. In fact she would start eating from her own bowl only upon receiving the command, "Eat!"

A holier than thou creature you couldn't imagine, who actually didn't speak unless she was spoken to. One never ever heard her bark, except on the command, "Speak!" The standard commands of "Heel, Sit, Down, Stay" were automatically followed. She would patiently play fetch, bring in the morning newspaper, and act as cushion, pillow, horse or whatever role was assigned to her. Gandhian by temperament, she did not know how to snarl. Being very gentle by nature, she would allow mice to play within her reach and even steal food from her bowl.

Her best friend was a stray cat, Hazel, who had adopted the family. They shared space, food and affection without rancour. On walks, Hazel would walk under Kola, weaving around between her legs. When troubled by other dogs or tom cats, she would send a special mew, which brought Kola bounding to her rescue, a lady knight in shining black armour.

Despite her gentle soul, Kola inherited the legend of the ferocious black beast, people vividly remembering her predecessor, Police, and mistaking one black dog for another. Her friendly nature, which made her gambol at all visitors with the intention of play, didn't help. Boy had to on one occasion rescue a visitor who climbed a tree to escape her friendly overtures.

The reader might remember a passage from Jerome K Jerome's immortal classic about three men, whose dog Montmorency looked so angelic that they wondered why she wasn't snatched off to heaven, till her behaviour exposed her. Kola looked and behaved angelically, and wasn't fit to remain in the mortal realm for long. A debilitating genetic disease, a curse of inbred kennel animals, brought her untold pain. Obedient and sweet natured to the last, she hopped onto the vet's examining table, submitted to all tests stoically, only whimpering faintly when the pain was too much to bear.

Boy was alone those days, his eldest in the hostel, and wife and kiddo in another city. At times he was lonely and depressed. Kola would sense it and forgetting her own pain, nuzzle him gently till he cheered up. She would patiently allow Boy to change her dressings, carry her out for her 'nature's call,' wash and brush her despite his natural clumsiness and ineptitude. But when she was off her biggest passion, food, Boy guessed the end was near. She waited till our whole family was together for a vacation, and surrounded by all, her head on Boy's lap, she left the unfair world of humans, convinced till the last that she was one.

Boy swore again not to have a short lived love again. Boy recently learnt that his little one has adopted a stray, keeping her secretly in her PG accommodation. And so the cycle starts again...

22

Marriage

Whenever a boy gets out of hand, the first solution that Indian parents think of is, "Let's get him married. That will settle him down." The hero of our story, Boy, is in a way my offspring, and has been getting troublesome of late. So I too, am planning the time honoured solution of getting him married off.

Boy met her in a dirty dingy government office, surrounded by mountains of dusty files, while peering out from behind huge ledgers to the background music of clattering typewriters. This was the pre-computer Stone Age of snail mail, manual computing, adding machines and files bound in tape holding typed letters. Find this difficult to believe? And no, there were no dinosaurs then, and the world wasn't black and white.

Hearing rumours that the presence of a young lady was about to improve the tone of the accounts department infinitely, Boy had gone to investigate. He returned crestfallen. The petite lady had actually made an appearance, and was to head the department, but Boy's breezy intrusion was met with a dead pan visage, and his attempts at witticism with a freezing, "Oh really, how interesting." Boy learnt later that he was just the kind of smooth talking long haired unreliable boy her mother had warned her about. However, as they were the only two non-geriatric beings in that vast dungeon, they sort of started to hang around together at lunch. It looked like other than being new recruits in this maze, they had nothing in common. Then one day, Boy found her solving a crossword puzzle and was elated. Pitching in, unasked, to help, Boy completed it to her mild irritation, but his skill with words must have impressed her a bit, as she seemed to thaw a few degrees. Finding at last that they had some common interest, Boy jumped in, and discovered that they shared a common passion for books, art house cinema and, although of drastically different genres, music. They began to relieve the tedium of work by exchanging books and cassettes, (remember those?) and news of exciting new writers, bargain prices for old books, or views on world cinema. Remember this was the pre- internet, Google, Wikipedia and social networking world, when knowledge and information were at a premium and the exclusive purview of the 'in' set. Boy was introduced to the melodious world of Hindi music, and he in turn exposed her to the disruptive world of Rock, and the mystical realms of Rabindra Sangeet. They progressed to visiting bookshops, Mandi House- the Mecca of theatre, and Shakuntalam- the auditorium for offbeat cinema. Next step, they became each other's confidants. Boy shared the woes of his latest unsuccessful attempt at a long term relationship, while she confided her problems in getting her dad to accept her unacceptable boyfriend.

Thus Boy learnt that she was of that rare species that was thought to exist only in Bollywood or Hollywood, one who was willing to do the unheard of naïve act of actually marrying for love, with no concern for Economics, History or Geography of the groom. Armed with this revelation, Boy took the only logical course, that of scheming to replace this undeservedly lucky guy.

At first she thought it was an attempt at comedy, and Boy's absolute inability to be serious about anything didn't help. However, Boy launched a marketing strategy of Perseverance, Irreverence, and Proximity. Brand promotion by his friends, and scientific product promotion helped by market feedback from her friends started wearing down her resistance, helped along by the jealous tantrums of Boy's predecessor. Finally, persuasion in the form of Psmith, who gets his Eve by telling her that the plus side of marrying a mad man is that you never get bored, swung the scales, to Boy's eternal gratitude to P G Wodehouse.

Now, in true filmy style, politics played spoilsport. Members of her community were being targeted in communal riots by people of Boy's religion. Her NRI dad planned her wedding with some suitable boy of their clan on the next available date. Her protests that she had other plans were peremptorily dismissed, especially when she produced a new candidate, this time, Boy.

The next logical step was elopement. While her dad was busy making arrangements for her quick disposal, they decided to close the deal. The registrar requiring some notice period, the Arya Samaj Mandir agreed to play cupid. They were assured that it was quite legal. Having no time to inform anyone or make any arrangements, they planned to meet at the venue the next day, get the certificate and promptly leave for Boy's hometown. Now more hitches made their appearance. Those were the days of long distance phone calls made from post offices where you had to shout out your messages in front of a waiting crowd, that too after waiting for an hour for the expensive 'lightning' call to materialize. After going through this trauma, Boy learnt that his father was abroad on work, his mother having accompanied him.

His school going brother's assurances that dad was returning the next day, and that Boy was not to worry but catch the train, or that little brother would take care of all issues, did not boost Boy's confidence.

By now, the jungle drums had spread the news, and there were a bunch of Boy's friends waiting with him at the temple, doing their best to add to his nervousness. Her delay was explained as second thoughts on her part, late realization of her blunder, her father having imprisoned her, or worse. Boy's worry was that a Wodehousian story shouldn't have a similar complication, where Boy waits by the Arya Samaj Mandir on Hanuman road, while she waits at the Hanuman Mandir on Arya Samaj Road. Another helpful explanation offered was that she gave him a subliminal message in her gift of a Talat Mahmood album, which speaks only of lost love.

In between, a subplot occurred where another bunch of Boy's friends organised the wedding at another venue, without the message ever reaching him. As there were no mobile phones and Boy was seldom at home, this wasn't surprising. Remember, this was the pre – SMS, WhatsApp, Facebook and email era. Thinking that Boy had changed his mind without informing them, they refused to speak to him for years afterwards.

Finally she arrived, explaining that she had to balance the books or some such office exigency, and ignoring the fact that Boy had aged a decade in the meanwhile. Quick ceremony over, certificate in hand, they proceeded to Boy's 'barsati,' a rooftop shelter that he shared with his friends – a typical bachelor pad of those days, familiar to all who have seen *Chashme Buddoor*. The plan was that Boy's bachelor roommates would move out, and she would move in. As Boy was completely broke, and she was leaving home with only the clothes she was wearing, his friends contributed to get them the basic furnishings and kitchenware to start a home.

Boy had warned his friends that he had neither the money nor the time to organise a party, so they volunteered to bring provisions. When Boy took stock, he found that everyone had brought liquid refreshments of various degrees of potency, and many had brought other aids for expanding the consciousness, but none had thought of getting food. A helpful neighbour produced eggs, sausages and bread, and a riotous party ensued. Leaving behind various comatose bodies, a few relatively sober friends managed to load them on to the train in time. En route to his home, Boy wanted to jump off at every station and head back.

At the station Boy's kid brother was there to receive them, but refused to disclose the situation at home beyond the enigmatic message that they would soon find out. A complete nervous wreck by the time he reached home, there was a sight waiting for Boy that he will never forget. The house was decorated in the traditional way to welcome the new bride, and relatives had gathered over for the ceremony.

Boy's brother explained later, that after his father's return and receipt of the news, dad had initially broken the world record for sitting high jump. But his next concern was for the poor girl whom his idiot son had gotten into this mess – she had to feel welcomed. So a traditional ceremony was organised overnight, with a diktat issued to all relatives that everyone was to be present to receive the new addition to the family. The patriarch's wishes were followed and a warm welcome was given to the girl from an alien culture.

Boy wished that he could be half the man his dad was, in showing love and support to his children when they really needed him.

So finally Boy is married off. But does this make him a man? Does our story end here? No dear reader, you don't escape so soon, for Boy has this Peter Pan complex, and refuses to grow up. There's more to come yet.

23

Caste

Boy's new bride was undergoing an interview with her grandmother-in-law. It was their first meeting. They did not share a common language so a bevy of eager aunt-in-laws were acting as interpreter. The favourite grandson had brought home a bride from a different community, so she was being magnanimous and getting to know the girl.

"Are you a Brahmin dear?" was the opening salvo to break the ice.

"No," her frank admission brought the chill back into the atmosphere.

"Umm, you are a Hindu though?" came the nervous counter query.

"No." Pindrop silence in the house.

Visions of the unthinkable unnerved the fond grandma and excited the eager aunts. A nervous follow up query finally emerged from the matriarch – "Um, are you, err.. a Muslim?"

There. The unthinkable was out in the open. The M word was out. Was a scandal about to rock the conservative bastion of the Ballygunge Brahmins? The aunts hoped for breaking news that would enliven their kitty parties for months. Grandmom feared the worst and only good breeding kept her from shifting away a little.

"No." Her reply dispersed the tension in the room. The old lady relaxed visibly. The aunts tried to hide their disappointment.

"Oh, so you are a Christian?" grandma asked, considerably relieved. Having been the wife of a civil servant in British India, she had seen a lot of Englishmen, who despite being Christian, were quite acceptable. Moreover, most of the family had studied in Christian schools, so they were not so alien. The previous generation who went to England for higher studies occasionally brought back a European wife, and although tut tutted at, they were tolerated. Basically, Christian was passé.

"No, I'm not," the bride replied.

"Then why did you scare us unnecessarily?" the beaming grandma retorted. "Not a Muslim or Christian means Hindu. So what if you are not a Brahmin, marrying one makes you one."

Feeble protests about Sikhs being a distinct community were lost in diffidence and translation. Relief, disappointment and vague frustration at a sudden loss of identity were the various emotions flooding the room.

It wasn't till a generation later that members of this community were at a wedding reception of the Ballygunge Brahmins as respected in-laws.

Unfortunately, the matriarch did not live to see that day.

24

Cooking his Goose

Boy was a foodie, and his expanding girth became testimony to it. He took a keen interest in the creative process of cooking too, but strictly in a theoretical way. He also enjoyed cooking as a spectator sport. The glamorous cooks on television made it look so sexy. However, the actual mechanics of it had eluded him so far.

Having grown up in the strictly feudal atmosphere of a Bengali bhadralok family, Boy had learnt to appreciate fine food without ever wondering about the process that creates it. Their kitchen was presided over by a family heirloom, the venerable Maharaj from a neighbouring state, who dished out delectable repasts à la Anatole of Wodehouse fame, but jealously guarded his domain, where even Boy's mother was denied entry.

When Boy finally left the comfortable cocoon of home and later hostel to venture out into the big bad world to forage for the daily bhat maach or pasta, this shortcoming became a problem.

He had moved into a barsati with some friends, a typical bachelor dig.

For economy's sake, for they were penniless bachelors, they decided to try cooking at home. The onus of providing dinner came by turns. When Boy's turn came he thought that khichuri would be a simple enough dish, as you could add rice, dal, vegetables, eggs, sausages, spices and everything one could think of in the pot with ghee and water and put it to boil for it to be done. The subtleties of proportion and timing and controlled heat escaped him.

The net result was that the mix turned black and started emitting a foul smelling smoke. Adding more water in a desperate bid to salvage the creation turned it into a thick black liquid broth. He dared not taste it.

Boy tried calling his creation Hungarian Goulash and tried it out on his most gullible roommate, but even he saw through it. Boy was demoted to procurer of ingredients, leaving the creative side to his more skilled roomies.

When Boy lost his single status and his partner moved in, his roommates moved out. Boy's wife was a superb cook, and his attempts to help out were quashed on the grounds of slowing down the process and leaving a mess in the kitchen. Boy's guilt regarding his inability, which forced her to juggle two difficult jobs – cooking the books at the workplace and a multicourse Bengali Punjabi fusion cuisine at home – continued to niggle, and they arrived at the compromise solution of hiring help in the kitchen, supervised by the LOH.

In due course, kids appeared on the scene, made life a delicious blur, and the years whirred past. Soon Boy had three militant feminists, who had allergic reactions to his feudal mores, running his life.

The fallout was that it was decreed that all of them would be self-sufficient, and at least make one meal for themselves.

Gone were the days of stuffed parathas in the morning, with generous dollops of white butter, which transformed Boy from a svelte youth into a rotund old man. The dictum was that everyone had to prepare their own breakfast.

The obvious answer was cereal with milk and toast and fried eggs. This Boy concluded would be well within his limited capabilities. Pouring the cereal into the bowl and pouring the milk on top was done without a hitch. The toaster popped up the toasts unaided, and spreading the butter was the toughest task so far, but he managed it without mishap. The first few days, he stuck to bread and jam, buttered toasts, sandwiches made from sandwich spreads and cereals soaked in milk for breakfast.

Now came the real test. Boy was attempting to fry eggs, sunny side up. He waited till he was alone at home. It looked so easy on screen. The pan is placed on the stove. A dollop of butter is plonked in, and starts sizzling and bubbling. Now with one smooth movement of the hand, the egg was cracked on the edge of the pan, to let the egg neatly drop in and magically turn into a golden smiley face. It looked so easy, elegant and stylish. And so the preparations were made. The hand holding the egg swooped in. Contact was made with the edge. So far everything had been going as per script, but now deviations set in. The pan leapt off the stove, the hot butter splattered Boy, and the smashed egg was all over the floor.

While Boy soaked under the tap and danced about in pain, his faithful Labrador cleared up the floor of the mess, shells and all, even cleaning the pan.

Undaunted, Boy geared up for attempt number two. He tried a less flamboyant method now. Pan, butter all in place, he held the egg over the pan and tried to crack it with a knife, to let the stuff plonk into the pan. It ought to have been really simple. But no, here too, things did not run as per script. The egg smashed and fell in the pan, shells and all.

After Kola, the lab, had removed all tell-tale evidence of the fiasco once again, a third attempt was planned. Robert Bruce tried seven times before defeating England we have learnt, but Boy had only six tries, limited by the number of eggs in the fridge.

This time the egg was broken into a separate bowl. After fishing out as many of the shells as Boy could, the egg was successfully poured into the pan. But the result wasn't the golden centre ringed by a white beach as advertised, but a yellowish white amoeba, brown around the edges, with bits of shell hidden inside.

Boy had discovered that ordering a takeout is best for anything more ambitious than bread and jam.

25

Karma

A friend recently shared with me the intriguing answers given by various American children to the question, "How do we know whom to marry?" This took me down memory lane to the time Boy's eldest had posed the same question to his wife.

He listened in for a while to the very sensible discussions between mother and child regarding getting to know a person and following one's heart, and kept having visions of his little child growing up and meeting all kinds of undesirable lumpen and following the very unsound advises of her heart.

He could also for the first time sympathize with his own father-in-law, whom till now he had considered an unreasonable ogre for his vehement opposition to his daughter's selection of a perfect boy like Boy for a life mate.

The venerable gentleman's objections were based on their different religion, language and caste, and not on Boy's qualities, character, education or socio-economic standing as a suitable groom for the apple of his eye – all of which Boy found unreasonable. Boy suspected that his pigmentation may also have had a bearing on the decision against him. Boy had cheekily offered to stop shaving and grow his hair if it helped matters, as a full flowing beard and unshorn locks were the hallmark of the community the pop-in-law belonged to.

What Boy realised now was that it was the natural caution of a doting dad to not care to lose his little girl to a smart-alecky stranger from an alien culture. Combined with this would be the very natural fear of the traditional middle class patriarch – "What would people say?"

Unencumbered by any such wisdom or scruples and armed with the arrogance of absolute certainty that is the prerogative of youth, Boy had eloped and got married ignoring his veto, no doubt bruising his ego, but also breaking his heart.

Now visions of Karma floated before Boy's eyes and life flashed before him in fast forward to the background score of 'Sunrise....Sunset....' He could visualize being introduced to young men in dreadlocks with piercings and tattoos or with orange hair, or perhaps someone darker than him with an afro hairdo, or maybe a skullcap and beard. Scenes from *'Guess who's coming to dinner,' 'Father of the Bride,' 'Meet the Parents,'* and *'Kanyadan'* flashed before his eyes and his sympathies were all with the beleaguered dads. He could totally understand Topol's anguish in *Fiddler on the Roof* as he watched his daughters leave without the aid of the matchmaker to impecunious youth, radicals and even a Christian! Now objections on grounds of race, religion, colour or creed didn't seem so outlandish.

Boy couldn't hold out any longer. Ignoring all homilies on good parenting, he interjected – "No, No! Don't listen to mummy, she doesn't know, I will tell you how you will know whom to marry; ASK DADDY! DADDY WILL TELL YOU WHOM TO MARRY."

Years later, when such discussions were close enough in time frame for the potential selection of a suitable boy to be serious, they joked about her childhood query and Boy's response. Boy tried to establish his liberal credentials by declaring that he didn't believe in race, religion or nationalities, but adding a rider for safety that socio-economic, educational and cultural compatibility leads to happier relationships. He jokingly asked whether he should fish out his dressing gown from storage and get a pipe, in preparation of upcoming interviews with young men à la fathers of brides in old Bollywood.

But the GenY lady's response had Boy completely stumped and re-evaluating his perceived liberalism. She asked Boy, "Does it have to be a man? Why this gender specification?"

I guess the young will always teach their parents new lessons in tolerance and adaptability.

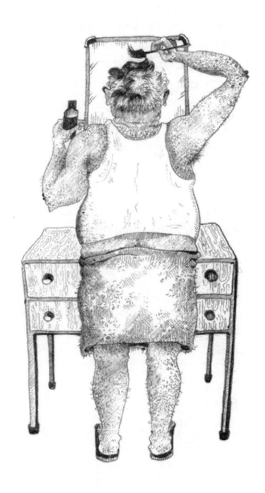

26

Age

"**A**ct your age!" How often have you heard this admonition? Boy has been hearing it all his life.

At first it was called "pakami," which means acting older than your age. Then it was called "chyablami," which is acting younger than your age. It seems he never got to act his age. When Boy was young, he would try to act older, and wanted to be considered an adult. This did not happen. But as Boy grew older, he wanted to be considered younger, and this did not happen either.

When you are in your pre-teens, a teenager seems all grown up, and a person in the twenties old. Those in their thirties are positively ancient. You club them with the geriatric set. Entering the teens, the same applies but with the shift of a decade. Preteens seem like infants now.

In the twenties this continues, only you now club teens with the younger children and consider them babies. We had a saying in our 20s – don't trust anyone over thirty. Back then you consider yourself to be in the prime of youth, and are busy trying to change the world, whenever you have time off from chasing girls. You are also desperate to lose your virginity, and add some substance to all the lies you told your friends about your conquests and prodigious feats in this field, half believing the lies your friends are telling you.

Now come the thirties, and you consider yourself the flower of manhood. By now you are married, probably a dad (or mom, but knowing the male experience firsthand I will restrict my story to that. It is quite similar for women from what I hear, except that they mature way faster than us). The anxieties regarding finding a livelihood, a partner and a place in the scheme of things, our little corner of the world, are over. This is when you are most confident and comfortable about your place in life.

Then it is the dreaded forties. All along you thought that these guys were over the hill. Now you are one of them! Children are older, expenses greater, finances tighter, partner less patient, career stagnating, belly beginning to bulge and grey streaks appearing in the thinning hair. You are desperate to feel young again.

Boy handled this dreaded birthday by joining a gym, colouring his hair, getting a new wardrobe and changing the model of his car. He took to teaching his daughters outdoor games in which he participated with more enthusiasm than skill. He also did a short course in rock climbing, rappelling and other such strenuous activities, and became an adventure sports enthusiast. He tried some very foolhardy stunts for a beginner and a middle aged man, but luckily survived without major injury or worse.

The gym phase lasted a month. The hair colour only speeded up the hair thinning, so was discarded, but led to the grey streaks turning into grey swathes. Despite strenuous efforts he soon became unable to give any competition to his daughters in swimming or badminton and they preferred spending the time with their own age group.

His wife took to gymming and stuck to it, and preferred to spend the time with serious fitness freaks rather than a huffing spouse. So Boy was back to spending the evenings lounging around the pool or the bar, with other middle-aged guys getting nostalgic for the good old days.

Finally the 50s came around. Panic struck. The dreaded F word!

Boy reacted by joining his wife's yoga class, which lasted a week; going on a crash diet, surrendered in a fortnight; quitting smoking for about a month; getting 'skinny' jeans and a wardrobe in line with the latest teen fashion, which never left his cupboard. He partied all night dancing to retro numbers much to the embarrassment of his kids, went rafting, climbing and trekking with kids half his age, did a road trip touted as among the most dangerous in the world although he had not driven for four years, and returned to herbal methods of expanding consciousness in desperate bids to recapture his youth.

Now his kids tell him to act his age.

But Boy is sure that he will be able to reverse time, and that the sixties will never happen.

27

Happily Ever After?

Recently at a friend's house Boy met a stand-up comic who strongly resembled the laughing Buddha figurines. He was brilliant in his repartees and had everyone in tears with his quips. He was accompanied by a very attractive young woman, obviously in love with him, and Boy learnt that she was defying family pressures to be his muse and life mate.

Boy offered them a piece of unasked advice, sharing a warning that his wife has been giving his daughters. To explain this shared wisdom, I have to tell a story.

In his early teens Boy was a bespectacled gangly boy, shy and nerdy, enthusiastic but ineffective at games, and absolutely addicted to reading. This did not make him popular among the boys of his peer group, and the girls he liked were all fictional.

For self-preservation in the jungle that is the teenage world, Boy used his facility with words as a substitute for brawn. Sharp repartee, wisecracks, ridicule and satire were his defensive and offensive weapons. This gave him a small measure of popularity and the school bullies kept a wary distance. But with adolescence, his soul cried for the company of feminine creatures outside the pages of books.

Boy's prayers were heard by some bibliophile god, and a neighbourhood kid he had played with as a child metamorphosed from a gangly awkward girl into someone who could be every teenager's dream girl. To the combined shock and resentment of the entire young manhood of the area, she adopted Boy as her official boyfriend.

Basking in the glory and warming in the heat of the jealousy of his peers, an emotion that was novel to him, Boy still could not quite believe in this miracle. What could the prettiest girl see in the ugly bookworm ignoring the hunks, sportsmen and the Richie Rich kids who usually monopolized the romance arc?

To unravel the mystery, Boy asked her. 'You make me laugh" came her honest reply. The secret unveiled, Boy blossomed into the class comedian.

Later they moved to different cities and drifted apart, but the mantra she taught him served Boy well. This message was later validated by his guru, Graham Greene, in whose *Travels with my Aunt*' the unprincipled uncle teaches the protagonist the secret behind his successful serial liaisons – 'You have to make them laugh."

This so became a habit with Boy that he could not be serious when required and the poems he tried to write turned out to be limericks. No one sought serious advice from him, job interviews provided entertainment to the interviewers but resulted in no jobs, and offering condolences in his flippant style would transform the grief of the grieving into rage, which could potentially get him killed.

By now Boy was looking for long term commitment in life, and was stuck by the fact that no one would take him seriously. The bright and personable young ladies would enjoy his company but would choose the serious young academics, budding bureaucrats or corporate cutthroats when it came to long term entanglements.

Thus when Boy met the lady he could not live without, she would not believe that Boy could be serious, and took his impassioned entreaties as more attempts at comedy. It did not help that she had been seeking relationship advice and Boy's solution was to replace her current flame with himself. Boy resorted to another guru, Wodehouse, and presented her with '*Leave it to Psmith*' to convince her of the serious intent behind flippant content.

Finally, the argument that clinched the deal was that the advantage of marrying anyone so obviously crazy is that you can never get bored. Ignoring saner counsel from all concerned, parental bans and cultural differences, she banked on a wisecracking clown and potential entertainment on long winter evenings for her future happiness.

In the decades that rolled by, Boy was blissfully happy, and presumed that he had kept up his side of the bargain, as he heard no complaints to the contrary. But then Boy heard her advice to his daughters as they reached the dating age: "Never marry a guy just because he can make you laugh. He might be funny now, but after 25 years, the gags will begin to get stale. You can bear the same joke only so many times."

This was the statutory warning that Boy shared with the couple at the party, who were giving him such a strong sense of déjà vu. He hopes they ignore it.

Are happy endings only in fairy tales?

28

Budget

Boy had to manage his own funds for the first time when he left home for college. The first skill he learnt in college was writing home for money. In those days money arrived by money orders. When this arrived, a notice was put up outside the hostel administration office. Expenses were always on credit.

From the canteen to the cigarette shop, chai wala and dhobi, everyone extended credit. The arrival of the notice brought them all to the door of their debtor, and chaperoned by them all, Boy would claim the money, clear his accounts and be left with nothing. So he would pick up the pen and start writing home for money afresh. How the money disappeared was a mystery he could never fathom, and the vicious cycle continued.

When Boy was gainfully employed by the benevolent government, he thought the problem would be solved. Four friends shared a flat for economy, and it was decided that everyone would record whatever they spent, and accounts would be cleared at month end, or whenever everyone was solvent.

Initially this worked fine, but as expenses continued to surpass incomes by a distressing margin, an analysis was done.

Immediately various objections were raised.

"How does auto fare get included in the common expenses?"

"How would I carry back the weekly groceries without a rickshaw?" came the retort. "And the nearest wine shop is miles away."

It was agreed that reasonable costs incurred towards procurement of shared commodities would be part of the common budget.

"When did you get toothpaste?"

"I brought it from home and all you guys were using it, so I added it to the costs," the cleverest roommate explained.

"But it was already half used," someone protested.

"All right, I will add a depreciated amount," this brilliant economist conceded.

Incidentally, this enterprising economist went on to become a millionaire merchant banker running his empire from an international financial hub.

"The kitchen and bar expenses are way too high, four of us can't be spending so much!"

"It's all the partying. We have too many guests eating and drinking us to bankruptcy."

"From now on, whoever invites a guest pays for them. We will add an extra man day per guest to him," the smart economist decreed. This was a complicated calculation involving the number of days each of them stayed in a month, adding extra days per guest, a calculation only the economist could completely follow, much to his satisfaction.

"Not fair!" protested the popular guy from the fashion industry. "You guys hang around flirting with all the girls who come to see me while I slave away in the kitchen! You guys can't talk to the girls in that case!"

So a compromise was negotiated. Male guests would be debited to the host member, while ladies were common guests and could be entertained from the common fund.

A while later Boy acquired a life mate, and his roommates moved out to make space for her in the tiny flat. This time it was truly a common fund and neither of them cared who spent how much on what. However, one aspect continued; they still could not make the funds last till the next salary, and were clueless where the money went.

They therefore decided to keep an account of all that they spent under various headings. At the month end an analysis would show where the cash disappeared. Upon auditing the accounts they found the two heads of accounts that were the guilty parties.

One was GK or God Knows. It was the money spent without the slightest recollection as to where it went, or the inexplicable gaps between cash drawn from the bank and pittance left after accounting for all the expenditures they could recollect. This mysterious Bermuda Triangle that swallows up their hard earned moolah continues to plague them to this day and they have agreed that this is one of the mysteries that are too complex for the human intellect to solve.

The other was Experience. Any absurd, unproductive investment or expenditure they made, like buying gadgets that did not work, or trying money saving methods that ended up guzzling their spare change (which they would swear they would never repeat again), they debited to experience.

Over the years they have learnt that experience is a black hole, it will swallow every penny they don't keep tied down, but give nothing back in return.

They finally decided to give up trying to balance the budget, and follow the national economy in deficit financing. This was made possible by two brilliant inventions, the credit card and the EMI. Now they do not have to live within their income, but earn just enough to cover the interest, as all major economies do.

Thus Boy has progressed way beyond those stony broke days in the hostel. Now there is no need to spend keeping short term earnings in mind, but with the hope of all possible future earnings. So Boy continues to live happily ever after in an ever mounting cycle of debt, certain of being remembered when he is gone.

29

The End

'Boys don't cry'
This is one maxim that made life difficult for Boy. Long before it was macho and cool for men to be in touch with their emotions and not be afraid to show sensitivity, Boy had the unfortunate predicament of being ahead of his times. He cried while watching films.

Not all films mind you. He did not cry during *Laurel and Hardy* films. But Charlie Chaplin was another matter. Action films left him dry eyed. But not if they were action packed patriotic war movies. Ditto action films to do with martyrs in the freedom struggle. These made Boy cry buckets. As did the first Hindi film he saw, *Haathi mere Saathi*. *Anand* left him cold, but *Fiddler on the Roof* was a three hankie film even before Boy had daughters of his own and identified with poor Topol.

This was his shameful secret. And it had to stay that way! If not quite his life, but his reputation and his young manhood depended on it. Cinema halls being dark, it kept a veil on this Achilles heel and no one suspected that the snivelling could be coming from the irreverent comedian that was Boy's public persona. His spectacles and the frequent colds he pretended to suffer from hid the symptoms of his shame from the casual eye, and Boy was as successful in keeping his alter ego a dark secret as Dr Jekyll. Books were another matter. Boy spent every bit of free time, in public transport and communal spaces as well, stuck in books. He would completely lose all sense of space time continuum when in the throes of this narcotic world, and would often laugh out loud or exclaim audibly. Giggles were frequent.

Now, while laughing aloud while reading is tolerated as eccentricity, with mild censure, and even giggling attracted bearable amounts of hazing, snivelling would have spelled a death knell. Boy's tastes did not run to soppy stuff, and tearjerkers made him laugh, so one would think that there was no danger of disclosure, but no, not quite. You see, what got Boy's tear ducts running were stories of triumph against odds, the little guy winning, the new kid scoring the winning goal, the 1911 Mohanbagan victory in the IFA shield in a real life *Lagaan* scenario and similar stories of heroism and success. Boy used camouflage in the form of loud laughter or eye irritation as a cover up.

But you can go only so far in covering up an overactive lachrymal gland. Rumours regarding his manhood began to circulate. It was only because Boy was an enthusiastic sportsperson, had the advantage of a scathing tongue and a reputation as a scrappy fighter that helped him survive those whispers. Not crying while in physical pain helped salvage Boy's name somewhat whenever he was beaten up defending his honour against any slur of emotionalism.

It was years later that Boy could openly cry with his daughters while watching *Lion King* or *Chak De India*.

One would expect that this albatross around Boy's neck would come to his rescue on the day he really needed the relief of letting his tears flow and wash away his anguish, thus unburdening his soul when something actually affected him in real life.

But like Karna's knowledge, the skill deserted Boy at his moment of trial.

Boy was keeping vigil in the loneliest place in the world, the waiting room outside the ICU. The one person Boy had hero worshipped in childhood, confronted in the arrogance of youth and grew distant from in the labyrinth of growing up, the one person who always supported Boy and was there for him without expectations of reciprocity, who's debt would forever remain unpaid, was inside, hooked up to a ventilator.

Boy was called inside and it was explained that there was nothing further to be done, and he had to take the final decision of flipping the switch. He was given a moment alone with the patient. Boy desperately waited for the welcome release of the warm flood that heals, but nothing came. He was dry eyed and stony faced. Boy went through the motions of bereavement in automation.

On the one occasion that boys can cry, Boy couldn't.

That day, Boy finally grew up, and became a man.

Tamam Shud

Epilogue

Nowadays, when savouring a good repast, the gourmet likes to enjoy watching the process. This is the era of open kitchens. I shall take a leaf from their book, and provide the same facility to my readers.

Here is a glimpse of the creative process for the loyal reader who has been following the story patiently so far -

Author, head tilted on one side, tongue slightly out, eyes squinted, typing laboriously with one finger.

Suddenly he looks up to see the screen blank. Curses a bit, goes back to menu – is clueless, calls someone and finds cursor had not been clicked at the right place. Starts again.

Occasionally he hits a wrong key or absentmindedly rests his elbow on the keys, or places the TV remote, beer glass, ash tray or the book he is reading on the long suffering keyboard.

(Note: author is an incurable multitasking addict – he is writing the story, reading Fay Weldon, watching *Anger Management* on Star World, has FB open on a browser, reading WhatsApp messages on his phone, sipping beer, eating chips, smoking and trying to keep the ash from burning holes in his Bob Marley T shirt.

Net result – strange messages appear or the writing disappears and large gaps appear in the script. Many entreaties later, his scornful offspring restores the original frame as if by magic and work proceeds.

A slightly tattered looking passage results, large parts of it in capital letters, paragraphs MIA, various red and blue squiggly things underlining the words.

Post the disgruntled daughter being cajoled into unscrambling the mess, the author discovers it is easy to create space, and that the squiggles are the red marks teacher used to put – for bad spelling and grammar. But opinion on spelling and grammar differs between computer and author, till the difference between American and English usage dawns on him.

But just before the happy ending, the screen goes dark and he discovers that the little message he was ignoring was telling him to add some power source, and the battery goes dead.

On the verge of tears, a charger is connected and after an eon of the heart stopping sight of a revolving wheel, the sign "restore screen" appears. Then there is excitement as the text reappears.

Clearly, it's not only Jesus who saves – Microsoft Word does too.

Now with some editing and copy-paste, a story is born.